Holy Ghost Stories for the Soul

Jo Hammers

Paranormal Crossroads & Publishing

Holy Ghost Stories for the Soul

ISBN 978-0-9849879-6-2

www.paranormalcrossroads.com

This work is fiction. All of the characters, organizations, and events portrayed in this novel are either products of the author's imagination or are used fictitiously.

TABLE OF CONTENTS

1. ON A WING AND A PRAYER   9

2. THE CALL TO COME UP HIGHER   15

3. UNCLE BILL'S BAPTISM IN THE HOLY GHOST   17

4. SISTER JEAN'S CALL TO THE MINISTRY   22

5. OUTHOUSE PRAYERS   25

6. WADING THRU DEEP WATERS   30

7. MY MOTHER'S MIRACLE   34

8. THE HISSING DEMON   38

9. THE LITTLE WAR PATH INDAIN   42

10. THE HOLY GHOST DEFLATES AN EGO   46

11. SINGING IN THE HOLY GHOST   51

12. THANK YOU FOR THE MIRACLE THAT IS ON THE WAY   54

13. MY TWO HEALINGS   60

14. SEND DOWN THE REINDEER LORD   62

15. THE LATTER RAIN AND THE BAPTISM IN FIRE   65

Dedicated to...

my daughter, Julie Jo.
May the Holy Ghost that set your
Grandmother's feet to dancing,
set your writer's pen a dancing too!

Jo Hammers

Holy Ghost Stories for the Soul

Jo Hammers

CHAPTER ONE

On a Wing and a Prayer

My parents were a praying on their knees, Holy Ghost filled couple. They would get up in the middle of the night and go pray for anyone that rang our phone that was sick or in need. Back in the 1940s and early 1950's there wasn't decent medical care for the poor and the free City Hospital was feared and seen as a place that the poor entered to die. It wasn't unusual for my mother to wake me up in the middle of the night and tell me to watch my little brother and sister that they needed to go pray for someone that was sick or dying.

On one of these occasions, my parents met a tall skinny independent Pentecostal preacher who was a guitar playing man. I suppose he was attracted to my parents because of their willingness to pray for others. He started to call on my parents, the first couple of times being in the evening about six-thirty. My parents assumed he was going somewhere to preach afterwards. He always left by seven. In those days church services started at eight o'clock at night. My parents always prayed with him and he would then leave.

At first, my parents were gracious Pentecostals and welcomed him when he showed up with his guitar to sit, play, and sing for awhile. My father played the Harmonica a little, so the music times at first were fun. Brother Clyde never failed to ask my parents to pray for him before he left. However, he would never divulge what he wanted prayer for. As time went on, Brother Clyde changed the times he started dropping by. He would show up at six in the morning on Friday, Saturday, and Sunday mornings much to my mother's dismay. That was not an appropriate hour to call in her thinking. But she kept quiet.

My parents met Clyde's wife Edinia eventually and their two small children. Edinia visited a time or two on Sunday afternoons, but not on a regular basis like Clyde. She worked full time. It wasn't long before my mother realized that it was Edinia that was working and supporting their family and that

Brother Clyde didn't work claiming to be a minister. My mother also began to wonder why Edinia had not embraced the Holy Ghost Pentecostal life of her husband Clyde. There were many unanswered questions in my mother's mind, but she lived in a day when the man was the head of the house and she never bucked my dad when he let Brother Clyde in. My father was supposed to head the house in her thinking. However, in the Holy Ghost power, my mother led our house.

My father was a little slow in seeing Brother Clyde as a non-working free loader and not a holy man. One day he would see, after my mother would be shown by God what his problem was. In the meantime, Brother Clyde continued to call in the mornings on Friday, Saturday, and Sunday mornings bringing his guitar.

On one particular Sunday morning at six A.M. sharp, towards the end of a year of his early morning visits, Brother Clyde showed up in a different car, a new late model convertible sports car. My baby brother, who was about ten at the time, was big into cars and spent hours at our kitchen table building models. Knowing that my brother was so interested in autos, Brother Clyde offered to take him for a short ride in his new chariot of fire, as he referred to it. My father let him go. My mother wasn't too happy about it, but she didn't say anything. My little brother went out and climbed in the passenger side of the convertible and brother Clyde climbed in the other side and they were gone about ten minutes. Then, Brother Clyde came flying back in to our driveway applying the brakes and squealing the tires which my father thought he had done to impress my little brother. This was the 1950's and hot rods and big engines were common subjects amongst men. My father saw the event as an opportunity for my little brother to ride in one of the horse powered machines of that day. Brother Clyde stayed outside in the car for a few minutes doing who knows what before re-entering our house. My brother jumped on out of the sports car and made his way inside all smiles.

"How was the ride?" my father asked my little brother expecting him to go on and on about the tire squealing, engine, or how it was a convertible.

"Well dad, you might say I was riding on a wing and a prayer." My little brother stated but said no more.

"My little brother hadn't made any major religious decisions at that point about religion. My father grinned thinking that perhaps Brother Clyde had preached to him for the whole ten minute ride and that was what my baby brother was referring to.

My brother went on in to the kitchen grinning, plopped down at the kitchen table for breakfast, and said no more. A usual round of guitar picking and hymn singing ensued and then prayers were said for Brother Clyde's unknown need and he went his way. My parents, at that point, were glad to just say a quick lip prayer to get him out of the house so they could get done what they needed to do. Their prayer bones were wore out with Brother Clyde.

My father was a hard worker and was adamant in his belief that a man was intended to work and support his family in order to be right in the sight of God. My father's God was not a welfare God and he didn't tolerate free loaders. To him, a man had to be respected as a man first and then in God.

My father often said, "A man who doesn't work and support his family is worse than an infidel!"

My father practiced those words and worked two jobs to support his family as well as getting up in the middle of the night to go pray for people.

The only exception to my father's thinking about men and their need to work manually for their bread was a minister. He felt a Holy Ghost filled man of God had his hands full praying for the sick and taking care of God's business. So, Brother Clyde, claiming to be a minister, was given a little slack in my father's eyes. Brother Clyde did say that he preached at some little church every week down in the boon docks about a hundred miles away. It was too far for my parents to go and Brother Clyde never offered to take them with him. So, my father just accepted Brother Clyde's story because there was no reason not to believe it. After all, Brother Clyde claimed to be Holy Ghost filled and Pentecostal. My parents were honest, so they just assumed everyone else was.

Sister Edina, Brother Clyde's wife, was always pleasant but didn't embrace the Pentecostal experience and I don't blame her now looking back. Her Pentecostal, guitar picking, preaching, supposedly minister of a husband was a nightmare to her, although my parents were oblivious to it. In my parents thinking, who were they to question who God had called to preach. They were just lay people in the Pentecostal ranks, prayer warriors and hard workers out in the laboring public.

My father worked two jobs and his main forty hour one was on the day shift. He rose at five in the morning. My mother hit the floor when the alarm clock went off and headed straight for the kitchen to make breakfast, coffee, and my father's lunch which she placed into his black metal lunch box. My father walked to work which was about a half mile from our house. There was no fast food back in those days. My father had to eat and then be at work at seven. He was never late. My parents were predictable, steady people.

On morning, just after becoming acquainted with Brother Clyde, he showed up exactly at five just as my parents flipped on the light. My parents didn't think too much about it although someone dropping in for a visit so early was unusual. They invited him in and asked him if someone was ill, the reason for his coming. He told them that there was no one ill, but that he just felt led to visit them. My mother poured him a cup of coffee and was gracious about it, even though his presence was waking up her children who needed to sleep another thirty minutes or so till she got my dad off to work. Afterwards, she would get them up, feed them, and send them off to school. School back then didn't start till nine. My mother was a very neat person, and it half way annoyed her that Brother Clyde would show up so early before she had her hair combed for the day. My mother had a set routine of doing things. Brother Clyde, who needed nothing, seemed oblivious to his intrusion. If it had been someone truly in need of prayer, my parents would have dropped everything, went and prayed for whoever needed help, putting me in charge of getting my siblings up and off to school.

One morning visit led to another and then another and another. The five o'clock visits in the morning became a regular thing with Brother Clyde. He would show up two or three times a week, especially on Friday, Saturday and Sunday mornings. He started asking for prayer and my father would lay hands on him and pray. My mother would stand praying. How could they turn someone down that was asking for prayer? They were prayer warriors.

After months of these visits, my parent's graciousness was wearing thin and they started not flipping their lights on at five. Instead, they would get up in the dark. My mother would close the door to her kitchen, close the curtains on her kitchen window, and then flip on only the kitchen light. This worked for a while. Then Brother Clyde started sitting in our driveway playing his guitar till six and then he would knock whether the lights were on or not. He was still oblivious to his being a growingly, obnoxious intrusion into my parents life.

A year and a half of these intrusions were wearing on my parents nerves. My mother kept telling my father that there was something about Brother Clyde that wasn't right. They had prayed for him so many times that my mother was starting to doubt her prayers. God just didn't seem to be in the answering business for Brother Clyde and they were in the dark as to what his problem was anyway. My mother didn't see herself as being able to pray effectively if she didn't know what the problem was, and brother Clyde was not divulging what his need was. He always had an unspoken request for them to pray for.

So, my Holy Ghost mother started to pray a new prayer every morning before he showed up. "God show me what his problem is and get him off of my morning door step."

My mother was confident that there had to be a reason Brother Clyde's need wasn't being answered. She hated to ask God to make him quit coming around, but she was desperate.

On the next Sunday morning, my mother was up trying to get us all fed and ready to go to church. A familiar knock came on the door and Brother

Clyde stood there holding his guitar by the neck. He was a little red faced. My father invited him in as usual. After he played a couple of hymns really sloppy, he asked for prayer. My mother had given up fervent prayers for him and quickly told him to stand in the middle of the living room floor so they could pray quickly and send him on his way. My father usually put his hand on Brother Clyde's head and prayed. On this particular morning, my mother didn't have time to wait on dad who was moving a little slow. She slapped her hand on Brother Clyde's head to pray with the intention of getting him quickly out of her house. She had a pan of biscuits in the oven ready to come out and she still had to make gravy to go on them. It was one of those mornings when you just don't have the time to put up with foolishness on any one's part.

After slapping her hand on Brother Clyde's head to pray, my mother was close enough to him for the first time to smell an odor coming from his mouth. Her brother Bill had been a bad alcoholic before he was filled with the Holy Ghost and became a minister. Her brother Bill never drank a drop after being filled with the Holy Ghost.

"Melvin . . . I am praying a new prayer this morning." My mother said pausing and removing her hand from his Brother Clyde's head. "Open the door and hold the screen door wide open."

My father assumed my mother was warm. It was summertime, there was no air conditioning, and she had biscuits baking in the kitchen stove for breakfast. He walked over to the door and did as he was told. He also considered the possibility that my mother had the intention of casting a demon out of Brother Clyde and sending it out into a herd of swine somewhere like Jesus did in the Bible. He held the screen door open and bowed his head so the demon, if there was one, wouldn't enter him. He started to pray in tongues to make sure he was okay in the sight of God. He knew my mother was capable of casting one out. My mother was the Holy Ghost filled power house in our family and my father knew it. Her prayers got answered. His did sometimes. So, he always followed her lead when it came to the moving of the Holy Ghost power.

Brother Clyde closed his eyes. My mother began to speak in tongues and in between said, "Thank you God for showing me what the answer is to his unknown request!"

Brother Clyde, with closed eyes, was expecting a Heaven sent experience getting my mother to pray for him. She had a reputation for getting things done in God's sight. Expecting my mother to give him the full Pentecostal prayer treatment, he smiled with his eyes closed and raised his hands. To his surprise, my one hundred and twenty pound mother grabbed him by the seat of the pants and the shirt. She then walked him on tippy toes to the front door, out onto the front porch, and then threw him off the front porch which had five steps to it and sent him a rolling.

A surprised six foot Brother Clyde jumped to his feet exclaiming, "Sister Marie . . ."

My mother walked back into the house without speaking to him and instantly returned with his guitar carrying it by the neck. She raised it in the air to smash it around our front porch post to the shocked face of Bro. Clyde. My father's face was a little surprised also. He had never seen a Holy Ghost woman speaking in tongues and smashing a guitar. That was a new one.

I think God let my mother find her righteous indignation point, just as Jesus did when he cast the money changers out of the temple.

The biscuits didn't burn that morning and the gravy was heavenly, the best she ever made.

As it turned out, Brother Clyde was an alcoholic who was trying to hide it from his wife. He drank heavy three nights a week in bars on Thursday, Friday, and Saturday nights. Those were the same three night shifts that his wife Edinia worked at a laundry doing sheets for hotels to support them. Those three nights also were followed by the mornings he showed up on my parent's doorstep. Keep in mind that there was no fast food back then. He would show up at my parent's house to get a cup of coffee and sober up just before going to pick her up at work. His unspoken request or need was to be sober when she climbed in the car.

Who knows where Brother Clyde's children were those nights and early mornings. They were young elementary kids. Edinia assumed back then that he was watching them. A guardian angel must have kept them thru all of those nights if they were home alone. There was not child abuse laws back then.

My parents realized at that point that the devil walks around in human flesh seeking who he might devour. The devil stalked my Holy Ghost Filled parents for one and one half years before my mother got victory over him. Brother Clyde did not preach three days a week down in the boondocks. He was a dark soul trying to use and connect himself to the light of God.

After my baby brother was grown he told of one wild ride in the convertible with Brother Clyde who drove seventy and eighty miles an hour around our town half drunk. When he almost missed a corner with my brother in the passenger seat, he laughed half drunk and said.

"We are riding on a wing and a prayer."

CHAPTER TWO

The Call to Come Up Higher

God calls men today to carry his word in many forms. Writing is my gift. I saw Christ as a child and he bid me to come up higher and walk in realms beyond that of ordinary men. I am one voice pointing men to the end time LATTER RAIN, the end time move of God.

I believe in the Baptism of the Holy Ghost with the evidence of speaking in tongues. I am not a Holy Spirit woman. I am a Holy Ghost woman. I also believe in a Baptism beyond the Holy Ghost, the Baptism of Fire.

I did not receive the Baptism of the Holy Ghost with the evidence of speaking in tongues till I was twenty years old. However, I received my call to a higher order in God when I was eight and in the night while I slept.

In the night in the land of dreams, I stood barefoot as an eight year old child wearing a yellow flowered dress looking up toward Heaven. Suddenly, a great ladder slid down from the clouds of Heaven with its feet landing and resting on the earth where I stood. I looked up and standing at the top of the ladder on the clouds was Christ in white arraignment. He extended his hands to me and called me to come up higher. He spoke without moving his lips. He then showed me that there would be many things on earth that would try to ensnare me and hold me from climbing the ladder. In the dream, I wanted to go with him right then and there. I was prevented from doing so. Then, I awoke knowing that Christ was real and not just a story my Sunday school teacher was telling. I have always been a person that questions everything. The dream was a prophecy to me concerning my future.

I never told my parents about my dream because I was a shy child and just wasn't a talker. I went thru twelve years of school with people referring to me as bashful or quiet. I was a called one, a child in the dry desert of human existence waiting for the end time latter rain to fall, for men to start climbing the ladder to Heaven and experiencing the latter rain or Baptism of Fire.

(Note: When I was about out of high school, my Aunt Golden, called my mother one afternoon really excited. She told my mother about having a dream when she lay down to take her afternoon nap. She dreamed of a great ladder coming down from Heaven and landing its feet before her. At the top of the ladder, Christ stood extending his arms down toward her. I had never told anyone about my dream, and hers was the same exact dream that I had seen. Aunt Golden was not Pentecostal at that time, but did embrace it after the dream. She was a member of the Salvation Army.

As a child, I was a thinker and stored treasures of thought and spiritual discoveries down deep in my soul. I was called to seek understanding that was not for the days of my youth but for many years in the future. The future has come and I am now climbing my ladder to him, experiencing my Fire Baptism and the promised end time LATTER RAIN.

This book is my attempt to share with you some of the stories of my family and friends concerning the Baptism in the Holy Ghost and the Baptism of Fire which is a baptism beyond the experience of being filled with the Holy Ghost.

CHAPTER THREE

Uncle Bill's Baptism in the Holy Ghost

My Uncle Bill was a tall, huge man weighing at least three or four hundred pounds. I never remember him weighing anything less. If you saw him heading your way for a visit, you quickly cleared a stout chair that was capable of holding him up.

My maternal grandmother, who was his mother, was the first in her family to join the Pentecostal movement and receive the Holy Ghost back in the 1930's. She was a middle aged adult woman with grown children when she first heard of the baptism in the Holy Ghost, an experience beyond salvation. At the time, she lived out in the country on a farm. One Sunday evening while she was doing some outside chores, she heard singing coming from the hollow next to her farm. Curious, she went to see what it was all about. As she neared, she said she heard the most beautiful sounds that she had ever heard. Following the voices that were singing in a language that she did not understand, she discovered a small revival going on in a grove of trees on the neighboring farm. In years to come, the gatherings in the countryside like she walked upon would be called Brush Harbor meetings. She took a seat, fell under conviction, and went forward when an altar call was given. After being saved, she returned to the Brush Harbor and tarried till she also received the Holy Ghost, an experience that she did not know existed ill she followed the voices.

One of her six children was my Uncle Bill. He was grown at the time of my grandmother's experience and was my grandmother's rebel or wild child. He was known to drink, fist fight, and was feared; someone you didn't want to mess with. Uncle Bill's nose was crooked and looked like a dog had chewed on it due to being in so many fist fights. In my grandmother's new Pentecostal faith, she learned about Holy Ghost deliverance and started praying for Uncle Bill to be delivered from his drinking, fist fighting, and sinful ways. She also asked that her headache child be filled with the Holy Ghost. Most of her other grown children just fell in line and followed her into the Pentecostal movement. My mother was baptized with the Holy Ghost when she was twenty -six or twenty- seven.

Pentecostalism back then was serious business and people lived what they believed. The women wore long hair, long sleeves, and long dresses. At church they gathered around the front of the church and prayed in the Holy Ghost till services started and then they had church. The religion being new, followers rented storefront buildings, met in brush harbors, and any other place they could throw in a few homemade slat benches and a handmade podium. The Holy Ghost was falling and the meeting places were packed.

Shortly after receiving the Baptism of the Holy Ghost, my Grandmother moved from the farm into the nearest city and started attending a small group of Pentecostals that were meeting in a garage that was originally built to house one auto. It had two wooden doors that swung out with handles on them and had a dirt floor. The building was sixteen foot wide and twenty-four feet long, about the size of some living rooms now- a- days. The garage church doors opened onto an alley. Most of the congregation walked to church which was common back then, even thought it was fifteen or twenty blocks. There was no insulation, wall board, or finished ceiling. It was what it was, a garage where Holy Ghost believers met.

In the cramped quarters of this twenty- four foot long garage, a single row of six, rough, slat benches ran down the center of the building with a small aisle on each end. Space was at a premium. You sat with your feet under the bench in front of you and your knees almost touching the backs of those sitting in front of you. The floor was dirt with sawdust scattered to keep people's shoes from resting in the dirt or mud. A Victorian, upright piano set up front on a small hand built platform to keep it up out of the dirt. There was a handmade speaker's stand and an altar built from rough unpainted planks. It was tight quarters in the small building and every inch of space was used. Chairs were stuck in any cubby hole available. Seating capacity was about thirty adults.

The rule of thumb concerned seating was, if there wasn't enough room for the adults to sit, you took your children off the bench and sat them down on quilt pallets in front of you or under the seat in front of you. Usually, every bench was always full as well as was the floor beneath the seats. If you were sitting in the center of one of those benches during services, it was almost impossible to get out should you want to leave for any reason. For one, there were too many kids on pallets to step over safely. Plus, it was considered rude to leave once services started. Everyone was told ten minutes before services to go to the bathroom if needed and to get a drink. Once the praying for services started up front, fooling around on anyone's part was over. Church was a serious business. The Holy Ghost was expected to move and you were expected not to.

It was fall and my Uncle Bill was well on his way to becoming drunk. He was stumbling about town looking for someone to fight with. Walking was common back in that day. Everyone got out and walked, even if it was twenty or thirty blocks. My mother and grandmother walked to church and it was many blocks from their house. On the night of my uncle's experience entering a Holy Roller church accidentally, my grandmother and his mother was sitting on the front row. She was a no-nonsense woman. Church was starting in the alley garage meeting place and only two seats were vacant in the whole place. She was a front row woman. The two doors of the garage were closed to keep out the chill of the evening. It was fall. Lights streamed out thru the cracks in the garage from kerosene lamps inside. The church was filled to capacity. Those in attendance were making a joyful noise singing, clapping, and making the little building they were gathered in vibrate with the Sounds of the Holy Ghost.

My uncle Bill just happened to be stumbling down the alley that the garage church faced. Like most drunks, he was just looking for a dark spot to sit down with his bottle and finish it off. He hadn't encountered anyone he could get into it with. As he neared the garage church, he heard music and thought it was the most beautiful voices and songs that he had ever heard. He wandered up to the two doors to stand, peep thru a crack, and listen. He had no intention of going in. As a rule, he stayed clear of his mother and her new religion that made you shout, dance, run, speak in tongues, and roll in the floor. He definitely was not a holy roller. However, in his drunken state, the music had his full attention. He could also hear someone singing in what was supposed to be tongues. He had heard his mother speak of it.

Just as he stepped up to one garage door to peep and listen thru a crack, it opened and a smiling man dressed in white stood there saying, "Come on in Brother. We have two seats left and one is yours."

Embarrassed about being caught peeping at the door, he entered. The man showed him to a seat third row from the front and right in the center of a bench. Uncle Bill had to step over kids, say excuse me, and cause a couple to stand up on the third row bench to let him in because he was such a big man. His knees actually rubbed the seat in front of him and the bench groaned when he sat down. On the other side of him, between him and the aisle on that side, sat one of the biggest women he had ever seen. Their combined weight was making their bench creak from stress. He definitely couldn't get past her if he wanted to leave that direction. He couldn't climb over her without making a scene. Her belly was so large that it was touching the seat in front of her. He was huge and she was huge. He took his slouch of a hat off and laid it on the empty seat next to him on the side where the couple sat.

Sitting there waiting for an opportunity, he noticed that the man in white had disappeared. He then plotted a way to get back out of the tiny church without causing a scene. His mother was sitting on the first row and he wasn't about to embarrass her. He was an adult, but he still lived at home. His intention was to wait till they all stood to pray. While everyone's eyes were closed, he would slip back out exiting in front of the couple. He was sure they would stand on the bench and let him out without too much fuss. He would whisper that he had to use the bathroom. There was no possibility of exiting the other way in front of the huge woman. Her huge belly and legs were pressed tight against the seat in front of her. He would pick up his hat and exit the other direction walking in front of the couple.

The singing ended and the minister started to take prayer requests. Uncle Bill sat still and kept his head ducked as everyone around him was holding up their hand and taking turns asking for whatever it was they had need of.

The preacher turned to my Uncle Bill, "And you brother, do you have a request tonight. Our God is in the granting business."

Sarcastically and in a half drunken mutter, my uncle answered, "An escape from Hell would be nice."

Just as the minister was taking the last request or two, one back entrance door of the garage church swung open and an extremely obese woman entered wearing a big hat. She made her way up the narrow aisle on the side of the building where the couple sat. Sure enough, the couple stood on top of the bench and pointed to the only empty seat where Uncle Bill's hat lay. Before he could think, the couple let the huge woman in and she took the tight seat next to him forcing him to scoot up next to the huge woman on the other side of him trapping him. Now, there was no way he could get out without making a scene and getting his mother on his case. He was not happy as the new huge woman then threw her arms in the air and began to pray in the Holy Ghost speaking in tongues and rebuking the devil. Her outburst spread to the huge woman on the other side of him and she also started to speak in tongues and threw her hands in the air shouting. Church was on. Someone started singing and Uncle Bill was in the center of the action with the whole church going wild with dancing, singing, praying, and the Holy Ghost of his mother making everyone around him do strange things. Then one of the huge women turned to him, slapped her hand on his back and started praying for him. She had him cornered and she had an in with God that he didn't. Instantly, he started to sober up.

Suddenly, his legs and feet started moving on their own. The woman on the other side of him rose and stepped out into the aisle. His feet and legs, that he couldn't control, carried him to the altar. They walked on their own without him telling them to do so. He had a Holy Ghost Pentecostal experience of someone moving his legs other than himself. Conviction fell on him, he prayed thru, and was filled with the Holy Ghost with the evidence of speaking in tongues. Then he stood to his feet and danced just like all of the other holy rollers in the church. God definitely got a hold of him. Uncle Bill was a lifetime shouter when the Holy Ghost fell on him; he couldn't control his feet and legs and would run the aisles of the church. The Holy Ghost made a runner out of him.

From that night forward, my Uncle Bill preached the Pentecostal experience and did so till the day he died. His testimony was:

"Thank God for Big Women and the Holy Ghost!"

CHAPTER FOUR

Sister Jean's Call to the Ministry

In the early 1950's, I had a friend who was about ten years older than me. I want to share with you what I recall of her words telling me how she was called to the ministry in a day when women ministers were not accepted. Jean was about sixteen when she started to preach as a Holy Ghost filled independent Pentecostal minister. Narrow minded male ministers looked down their bent noses at her and she preached their bent noses out of shape.

There was no possibility of Jean obtaining a position as a church pastor back then. That did not matter to her. She created her own pulpit. Finding an old storefront building in the poorest part of her city, she rented it and erected a hand lettered sign reading "THE STRAIGHT AND NARROW Pentecostal Church". She never had a professional sign painted in all the years I knew her. If she needed a sign, she got a board and a can of paint and then lettered a sign of whatever she needed including the church meeting hours and her name as pastor. It didn't matter to her if the lines of lettering on her signs ran a little crooked up or down. It was God she was interested in, not frivolities such as expensive signs.

Just before turning sixteen, Jean had been attending a Full Gospel Church in a little mom and pop storefront. It was common for Pentecostals back at that time to ask everyone to come to the front and pray for service. The altar in the little storefront mission was full, so Jean took a position on the side at a slat back bench the ministers usually sat on during service. Others joined her on their knees there. In those days, everyone but the sinners prayed up front before services. If you didn't, you were considered backslidden. On the night I am speaking of, the front of the church was full of knelt people praying.

Back then, flowery prayers weren't said. People moaned, groaned, and got down serious with God asking forgiveness for their own sins before starting to pray for the service. It wasn't a time of sitting on fancy pews in fancy dresses trying not to wrinkle your dress or pants till the service was over waiting for a wimpy Holy Spirit to sweep over you gently, so as not to wrinkle your look. People sat or knelt on rough, uncarpeted, wooden floors and prayed in unknown tongues for twenty minutes or so asking God to come and be in their midst for the service and for the HOLY GHOST to move and have his way.

Poor men of the time wore overalls and were lucky to own a pair of dress pants. There were no food stamps or commodities back then. Poor people struggled just to feed themselves. My own family ate fish, squirrel, whatever my father could come up with to supplement our diet of beans and potatoes. The poor of the city lived in tar paper shacks and many had dirt floors. If you happened to work for the railroad and could live in one of their three room shotgun houses, you were considered prosperous amongst the poor. The railroad housing in our city was named Yellow Row because the houses were all painted the same color. None of the houses had running water. Everyone carried their water from a company water faucet. Women did their dishes in dish pans, toilet facilities were out houses, and you bathed in a round wash tub. It was the poor people that needed hope and Jean would become their minister.

When poor people went to the hospital back then, it wasn't to get well, they expected to die. Everyone feared going to the free City Hospital. It was basically a free nursing home that you entered when you were at death's door to die in if you were poor. So, healing amongst the Pentecostals was prayed for seriously, not a wordy prayer taught to children to do lip service. Healing and food were entirely up to God, because the poor had no medical coverage, money in their billfolds, or food in their pantries.

Jean was a Holy Ghost and Fire believer as a young girl. On the particular night of her calling, she was on her knees at a slat bench on one side of the front praying with the other congregation members for service. She opened her eyes feeling the presence of someone and looked about. Across the room stood Christ with his hands outstretched bidding her to come to him. She turned on her knees and faced him. She could not rise to her feet because of his holiness. She crawled towards him across the front of the church passing the altar of praying men. She crawled with one hand extended upward reaching out to him. Halfway across the room crawling to him, she heard him speak.

"Jean. . . "He called. "Will you work for me?"

"Yes, Lord! "She answered thru a flood of tears in a crawling position as she continued to crawl towards him. He was like a magnet drawing her to him. She wanted to touch him, to just touch the hem of his garment."

"Jean . . ." he called again, "Will you feed my sheep?"

"Yes, Lord!" She answered again reaching out to touch him.

"Jean . . ." he called again. "Will you preach my word?"

"Yes, Lord," she replied sobbing.

"Straight is the way and narrow the gate, Jean. Enter into my calling! Preach to the poor, witness in the streets and alleys. Shame the men of your city. I have called many of them and they have not answered their calls."

Then Christ disappeared and Jean lay on the floor of the Pentecostal Mission weeping. She had been called to preach in the Pentecostal ranks by Christ who didn't care if she was a woman.

Jean became an independent lady minister in an era when women ministers were not accepted in main stream religions or even in the Pentecostal ranks. She had to create a world and life to serve her Christ in. When you have been touched by the Master or had a visitation from him, there is no turning back or listening to narrow minded men say you cannot preach.

Jean found herself a job and faithfully took her wages and paid the rent on a storefront building where she established an independent Pentecostal Holy Ghost church, lived in its back rooms, and was faithful to her calling for a life time. She preached on streets, in alleys, in tents, on the radio, and wherever God opened a door for her. She was a no frills woman who didn't even have a bookmark for her bible. In her last days, she would take clip-clothespins and mark where she was to turn in her bible next when she was preaching. She worked a regular job for over forty years and took her wages and paid the rent on a building in faithfulness to God and her calling. She ignored the men who told her she couldn't do it or that she wasn't called. She knew better.

Are you a book mark person or a clothespin one? Are you a Holy Spirit person or a Holy Ghost one?

CHAPTER FIVE

Outhouse Prayers

My father and mother loved to go to tent and other types of revivals. In the summer time, in our city back in the 1950s and early 1960s, it was common to have a couple tent meetings a year arrive and set up in a field north of the city.

By the early 1960's, city codes were being passed and our city started requiring the tent revivals to have a Portable-John for the men and one for the women. In the 1950's provisions such as that was not provided. Before the 1950's you just automatically knew when you went to a tent revival that you had to use your own home facilities and make your kids use them before taking off to the meeting. There would not be a chance to use restroom facilities again till you got home two or three hours later. It wasn't unusual for my mother to line us kids up the last five minutes before we went out the door to make sure we made it thru the meeting and arrive home without wet pants.

In the Early sixties, Portable Johns started to appear at the tent meetings and the lineups at home started to cease.

The portable restroom facilities had a lock on the inside of the door so you could use the facilities in private. On the outside of the door they had a barrel latch which could be pushed closed to hold the John's door closed during transport back to the John company to be emptied and cleaned. It kept the door from flopping during transport.

My father and mother had made a new set of friends who had custody of their little red headed grandson who we will call Dustin. He was a fiery little live wire and what he couldn't get into couldn't be thought of. He would have been diagnosed as hyperactive, had it been today. Back then, he was just referred to as a handful. He and his grandparents accompanied my parents just about everywhere. My parent's last son had just left for the army and they were free to get out and move about. They went to church some-where almost every night of the week.

My father's name was Melvin and my mother's name was Marie. Their friends were called Junior and Annie.

A huge revival tent had been set up in the vacant field north of town. It was rumored that the evangelist, who no one knew, had the gift of The Word of Knowledge and called people out prophesying to them. News of the coming of the Holy Ghost filled Evangelist with the Gift of Knowledge spread thru the Pentecostal community. Everyone was looking forward to the prayer line he was rumored to be going to have. The Word of Knowledge was consid-ered at that time to be the highest gift to be given by God.

My father was excited and couldn't wait for the evangelist's sermon and to possibly beat out the crowd and get a near front position in the evangelist's prayer line. He planned to sit on a certain side of the tent in a certain row so that he could get in the prayer line and be one of the first ten or twenty prayed for. Perhaps that was a little bit of greed on the part of my father. He wanted to make sure the evangelist ministered to him before he became tired and possibly quit. Keep in mind that my mother was the powerhouse in our family and had the Holy Ghost connection. My father always seemed to have some sort of agenda to everything he did. He had it planned how to beat the pack of his Pentecostal brethren and be one of the first in line. My mother was happy to just raise her hands where she was seated, praise God, and let Him have his way in her. My father was an agenda man with God.

So, my father and mother made their way to the tent early and claimed their chairs. Junior and Annie with grandson Dustin met my parents there and were agreeable to sit where my father had chosen.

It was about three minutes till service was supposed to start. Suddenly, my father's stomach started to roll and he nudged my mother.

"I can't help it. I am going to have to make a quick trip out to the portable John. Don't let anyone have my seat, I will be right back." He whispered.

This wasn't really too acceptable in my mother's opinion. They had for years made us kids go before church and after church only. He and his stom-ach were breaking the rules. She didn't smile, but she didn't say anything. After all, their kids were grown and none of them were under the tent to see.

My father left the tent heading for the portable- John. A light breeze sud-denly blew up sweeping thru the tent blowing anything lightweight and loose around. The men in charge of the setting up and taking down of the tent let its curtain flaps down on the side where the Men's John was to block the breeze. Little did they know, it was the breath of God moving in a strange way causing them to put down the curtains on just one side of the tent hiding the view of the Porta-John. God was about to teach someone a lesson. It was hot summertime and there was not a breeze blowing anywhere else. So, the portable-John became out of view and hearing of those in the tent.

Dustin, seeing that my father had been allowed to leave and go to the outside toilet facility, suddenly insisted that he had to go just about the time the song leader stepped onto the platform and asked everyone to stand and pray for service. My parent's friends didn't want to miss out on anything, so they whispered to Dustin to go straight to the Portable-John and straight back.

My mother frowned again. However, it wasn't her child and not her responsibility to force him to wait. She kept quiet. What could she say when her own husband was breaking the rules.

Red headed Dustin ran down the aisle, out of the tent, and disappeared beyond the flaps down side of the tent and out of sight of his guardian grandparents.

The service began and the music was fabulous. A huge Hammond organ was belting out revival music drowning out any other sounds for the evening. People started raising their hands and letting God move. My mother, who usually closes her eyes a lot during church services, got lost in the Holy Ghost and was unaware that my father had not returned.

Meanwhile, out in the area where the Portable-John had been placed, six year old, red haired Dustin walked up to the John's door that had a man's figure on it and tried the handle. A familiar voice came from beyond the door.

"Give me just a minute, I am about done." My father's voice stated politely.

"Is that you Mr. Melvin?" Dustin asked crossing his legs having to pee. His grandparents had not made him go before he came.

"Is that you Dustin?" My father inquired from inside the portable outhouse.

"Yes, hurry up! I have got to go bad." Dustin replied squirming.

The music and the sounds of people praising God was starting to pour out from the tent. However, inside the Portable-John, which was a plastic like structure, the sounds were just muffled noise. The music could be heard somewhat but not the voices praising God.

"I need just another minute or so Dustin. I have a belly ache." My father stated nicely thru the door and then suggested, "Try the women's restroom. They won't mind."

"Oh . . . , okay! " The red headed little spit fire stated as he suddenly discovered the barrel latch on the outside of the John's door. He ran his fingers over it trying to figure out how it worked. He slid the little long bolt back and forth on the door trying to get it to go into the chamber on the frame of the structure. He continued playing with the slide bolt a moment longer thinking that Mr. Melvin would come out sooner or later. However, Dustin's full bladder and crossed legs won out. So, he abandoned his fascination with the barrel latch after successfully getting it to enter the round hole to lock the door from the outside. Then he headed for the women's Portable-John and quickly used it not locking or closing the door. When you have got to go, you have got to go. After using the women's facility, he made a run back to the inside of the tent because stinging mosquitoes were after him. He figured the little blood suckers couldn't bother him if he could make it back under the tent where the lights were. Once inside, he flew down the aisle and sat down on a folding chair next to his grandparents and became fascinated with a man that was playing a guitar and singing upon the platform. Mr. Melvin, who was locked in the Portable –John, no longer had his attention. Dustin was a hyperactive little boy with a short attention span and had simply moved on to something else.

My father finished his business in the Portable-John feeling he had only missed maybe five minutes of service. He was in a hurry to get back and not miss out on anything further. He pushed on the door to exit and it didn't open. He pushed harder and it didn't open. That was when he realized that he was locked in. He began to yell for Dustin thinking he was still out there to let him out. Dustin did not answer. He rattled the door and yelled loudly thinking someone had to be out there to let him out. No one came to his rescue. The curtains that had been let down were shielding him and his voice from the workers. The workers kept the tent standing and usually walked the perimeter of the tent watching for pranksters or anyone who might want to harm the evangelist or cause problems. On that particular night, the Holy Ghost was moving and all of the workers were standing and praising God inside the tent.

After fifteen minutes of frustrated yelling and trying to get the lock to give, my father realized that no one was coming possibly till service was over. He remembered all the years he had made his children wait. He didn't know whether to pray for help or to repent. God had provided him with one smelly altar, a John full of urine and excrement. Everyone had used the John early to make sure they wouldn't miss out on any part of the rumored service that was to be the best for the summer. My father was up a creek without a paddle as they say. The music was drowning him out and there was no hope of anyone letting him out. He sat down on the John stool and waited for someone's bladder to eventually have a spasm and discover him being locked in.

Out in the Portable-John my father prayed a new prayer.

"Oh God . . . Please hear me in this plague infested, portable-toilet and send someone to rescue me." He didn't think he was going to be able to survive the smell. Not only that, but mosquito were starting to come thru the air vents in the roof. Then the worst of Mr. Melvin surfaced and he continued his prayer. "Please help me not to kill that red headed, little Devil who locked me in this Hell."

Finally an elderly man's bladder sang and he headed for the portable John. He wore hearing aids in both ears and was basically deaf. The old man intended to just step behind the john and do his thing. His knees weren't too agile and he was afraid he might not be able to rise easy if he sat down on the low stool in the John. My father heard something stirring and he hoped it was a man and not a dog. He began to yell. My father was lucky the old man heard him. Perhaps the Holy Ghost felt my father had enough discipline and healed the old man's ears. The Holy Ghost can do anything.

Once out of the John, my father made a run for the tent and then was embarrassed when every eye turned watching him as he walked in extremely late and took his seat next to my mother. Everyone that knew my parents were aware of their feelings about people who left services interrupting it or entered late interrupting it.

It was not till many months later that my father admitted that he had been praying for patience. He said patience was one virtue he would never pray for again. Sitting in a poop and urine filled Portable-John with gnats, flies, and mosquito biting you; waiting for someone to rescue you like Daniel in the Lion's Den was not a pleasant patient lesson to learn. He became a Daniel in the lion's den fan after his experience.

Everyone raved what a great night in God the tent service was and how the Holy Ghost had moved and people were blessed. My father grinned, but he had no comment. He was practicing self control. Dustin was standing next to him under the tent after service while everyone was saying their farewells for the evening.

My father had missed the prayer line because the evangelist held it before he spoke instead of after.

"Did you figure out how to work the door, Mr. Melvin?" the red headed, six year old asked my father as he stood with him after service. In his six year old thinking, there had been no problem. Grownups could open anything.

God met with my father that night in a special way, but it wasn't in the way that he expected. The Holy Ghost fell inside the tent and my mother who was a Holy Ghost dancer was blessed. The Holy Ghost also moved inside the men's portable John teaching my father a lesson in patience, practicing what you preach, and not to have a greedy agenda.

CHAPTER SIX

Wading Through Deep Waters

Even though we Pentecostals believe in the move and power of the Holy Ghost, we are human and sometimes ordinary things happen in church that we have to laugh about.

In the late 1960's, my mother and I attended a snowy night, winter revival held by a woman minister everyone called Sister Boyd. We drove down in the hills of the Ozark Mountains where only a person packing a gun could possibly have lived. At that time, the area was rumored to still have cougars, bears, black panthers, copperheads, and rattle snakes. On the way driving there, a black panther ran across the two lane highway in front of us. I was in my twenties at the time and sort of into women's lib. I believed that a woman should try to be all that she could be and I respected this woman minister who was bucking the male establishment and holding revivals all over southern Missouri. Women ministers at that time were looked down on. I was doing my bit for women's lib and supporting her. That was my main reason for going.

It was winter and there was an icy snow on the ground. It felt good to get inside the small church, a converted house and get warm. The wood stove that was heating the place was doing its thing and I relaxed removing my coat. My mother did the same. The inside of the small house church had its center partitions removed with a couple of poles supporting the ceiling. We sat on a wood slat bench. Our seat suddenly started filling up making us slide toward the wall. Only a center aisle existed. We basically were blocked in till after service ended. That was okay with us. We had no intention of going outside, braving the cold, and possibly get eaten by a bear walking to the church's outhouse.

Sister Boyd was a believer in miracles and she pulled bigger crowds than most any independent male evangelist in the area. There are always sick people with needs and people with other types of problems that need help. She seemed to have an in with God and people flocked to her.

Sister Boyd played the guitar and when she got up to preach, she would close her eyes, speak a few words in unknown tongues of the Holy Ghost and then start to pick her guitar and sing. As she sang, when there was a pause, she would speak in tongues, and then go on singing. There was no doubt that God was going to move because it was already moving on her.

Pentecostals are big into singing choruses when the Holy Ghost is moving. Power in the Blood was a popular revival song back then as well as one that talks of the Holy Ghost sweeping over your soul. I could tell that the congregation was going to be a praying, chorus singing, dancing one. The Holy Ghost was already moving on Sister Boyd. People were raising their hands in praise and the building full of believers was just about to come alive.

On that particular night, my mother and I sat with our feet underneath the seat in front of us because the hand-built slat back benches were close together. When you stood, your stomach was totally against the seat in front of you as you clapped and sang during the lively song service.

My mother who was in her late fifties at the time had on a pair of little green cloth topped shoes that were sort of a felt material. She always wore a dress and nylons. Pantsuits or pants for women were considered a sin in those days. My mother was dressed appropriately; even though it was a cold, snowy, night. I was dressed appropriately also.

My mother carried an old fashioned floral handkerchief with two quarters tied in the corner of it. If the Holy Ghost moved and she needed a handkerchief for tears, she had one. When it was offering time she had her donation ready. So, my mother sat prepared next to the wall listening to Sister Boyd start to sing, speak in tongues, and call for God to send his Holy Ghost Power down. We listened as Sister Boyd stopped playing her guitar for a moment and spoke to the packed house.

"God is getting ready to move, but I feel that someone is going to have to wade some pretty deep waters tonight trying to get home. Everyone be prepared, because it might be you. Let us all sing now the chorus 'WADING THRU DEEP WATERS TRYING TO GET HOME'. I personally am stepping into the deep waters of God willingly. If you want the power of God to fall on you tonight, I want you to step into the deep waters as they begin to fall and let them wash over you."

My mother was sitting with her eyes closed preparing to enter into the service and let the Holy Ghost have his way with her. She was willing to wade into the deep waters. My mother was a shouter, a dancer, a tongue speaker, and a woman who would raise her hands to join in on whatever the Holy Ghost and God was dishing out for the evening. She raised her hands holding her handkerchief in one hand and started to worship. Sister Boyd spoke in tongues and began to sing the chorus which was a repetition of basically one line of thought.

"I am wading thru deep Holy Ghost waters trying to get home.

I am wading thru deep Holy Ghost waters trying to get home.

I am wading thru deep Holy waters – I am wading thru deep Holy waters –

I am wading thru deep Holy Ghost waters trying to get home."

Sister Boyd just kept singing the chorus over and over.

It was not unusual in Pentecostal services for mothers to lay sleepy toddlers down on pallets underneath the slat bench seats or on top of one if the room wasn't needed for someone to sit. There were no nurseries back then. Children stayed in the night services and fell asleep to the music when it started. One little boy about three or four in front of us had been yawning earlier and his mother lay him over on the bench beside her and directly in front of my mother. He was asleep before the song service started. His mother closed her eyes entering into the service and didn't think to cover him up. He slept there uncovered while Sister Boyd sang her repeated chorus about the deep waters. My mother's feet were under his section of the seat. She also had her eyes closed entering into the service along with Sister Boyd and the others in the building.

"Come on . . . "shouted Sister Boyd suddenly shivering underneath the anointing. She proceeded to speak in tongues and then once more entered into the same deep waters chorus. "Sing it out . . ." She shouted and continued.

The crowd was coming alive and my mother had her arms in the air doing a little Holy Ghost wave thing. We were all seated for the moment, but hands were being raised and there was some shaking going on as the Holy Ghost moved over the congregation. There were tears rolling and a couple of short outbursts of tongues. The rest of us were getting with the program singing the chorus and starting to move our feet to the beat. I knew my mother's Holy Ghost dancing feet would bring her up off the bench she was sitting on at any moment. I knew her.

Suddenly, my mother lowered her hands, turned and looked at me really strange and snickered. I didn't have a clue what was going on, but snickering wasn't usually how the Holy Ghost moved on my mother. I leaned over to her so she could whisper in my ear. I knew something was up, but I didn't know what.

"Why are you laughing?" I whispered. I had been thumped on the head a few times when I was young for laughing and cutting up in church.

"I really am wading thru deep waters trying to get home." She whispered back and pointed to her feet.

I quickly looked down at her feet. The little boy who had fell asleep on the seat in front of us had wet his pants and the urine had flooded down thru the slat bench underneath him and drowned my mother's feet in her little, green, felt cloth shoes.

Then I snickered. I was sure that my mother was the one Sister Boyd had seen wading thru deep waters trying to get home. Sister Boyd's prophecy had come to pass. She had seen it before it happened.

My mother's feet were drenched. She took her handkerchief, which was usually used for her eyes when the Holy Ghost moved, and wiped away the deep waters that had fell on her legs and feet. My mother got a new pair of shoes the next day. There was no way of washing the little felt numbers.

On my mother's death bed she spoke of being able to see Mark and Luke, Jesus' disciples, standing and waiting to walk her over. No matter what comes your way, wade your deep waters and keep on wading them till you cross over to the other shore. On the other side, you can remove your water waders for a pair of NEW SHOES and then shout and dance all over Heaven in them.

This is one of my most treasured moments spent with my Holy Ghost filled Pentecostal mother.

CHAPTER SEVEN

My Mother's Miracle

About 1950, my mother developed a huge lump in her breast and was frightened to death of dying and leaving us as a family to fend for ourselves. I had three older brothers and I was her smallest child, a girl who hadn't started school yet. My mother was Pentecostal and wanted us raised according to her standards which were somewhat higher than my father's, although he was a good man.

Although both of my parents were Holy Ghost filled Pentecostals, it was my mother that was the keeper of the faith and the one that God spoke to in our family. My father spoke in tongues and was a believer, but it was my mother who read her Bible, prayed, and prayed for others.

Huge Tent revivals were popular back in the days when I was small. Famous evangelists came thru my home town every year. The evangelists came in a variety of faiths and persuasions. My family's belief system was Pentecostal and we as a family attended the Pentecostal revivals. The Tent Evangelist that came thru Springfield at the time my mother had a huge lump in her breast, was an evangelist known as Jack Cole. He was a healing evangelist.

It was on a weekend back around the year of 1950 that my parents made their way to a gospel tent erected in a familiar, dusty field to hear an evangelist they had never heard of. Night was falling and my parents sat patiently in their car waiting for service to begin. Services back then didn't start till eight o'clock at night. Cars were pulling in and it was evident that there was going to be a huge crowd. My parents had heard the man drew large crowds in other cities and they made sure they were there early and had a parking spot.

My parents were always early for everything. Being late was not an option to them. They paid their bills on time. They arrived on time. My father got up and ate his breakfast and went to work on time. They lived their lives on time. They were steady honest people. Being a little early, we sat as a family in our car till it was about time to claim a seat beneath the tent.

Mom let my three brothers out of the car to run and chase fireflies with some other kids that were passing time before the healing meeting started. She had a purpose in letting them go do that. She needed to speak with my dad and I am sure what she wanted to speak of was not considered a proper subject to discuss in front of my brothers or men back at that time. I am sure they thought that I being so young was oblivious to what they were speaking of.

"Melvin . . . ." my mother said leading in to a conversation with my dad.

"What Marie?" he answered watching men roll up the flaps on the huge gospel tent letting people enter.

"The lump in my breast is larger. I am going to get in the prayer line tonight. If God doesn't help me, I am going to die. I want you to put your hand in my blouse and feel the size of the lump so you will know that God has healed me when I let you feel the place after I have been prayed for."

My father did so ignoring me.

"It is the size of a small egg . . ." he stated in shock looking at her in the dark of the car. It was at that point that my father knew how serious my mother's problem was, as well as the fact that he was possibly looking at raising his four children alone.

"I just wanted you to know." She said.

After the conversation, my parents got out of the car and walked under the tent to participate in the healing revival. My parents found seating for them, me, and my brothers. The folding chairs were wooden.

I don't remember much about the service except the long line of individuals that my mother stood in to get prayed for. My father kept the four of us children under control while she did so. I sat and watched. My brothers were more interested in crawling around in the sawdust aisle next to us playing. Perhaps it was the fact that it was my mother up front that I sat so patiently and watched the healing line. Most little kids don't want their mother out of their sight for very long.

There were probably a hundred or more individuals in the line and my mother was at least half way back in the line if not further. I remember the minister praying for a man about a third way thru the line and the man getting excited telling Evangelist Jack Cole that a huge tumor, a knot in his stomach, had instantly disappeared when he was prayed for. I remember the people under the tent getting excited and praising God and the healing line continuing.

When my mother got to the healing evangelist, she lifted her hands to Heaven. He put one hand on her forehead and prayed which was a common way for a Holy Ghost filled Pentecostal minister to pray for a woman in those days. When he was finished praying, he removed his hand from my mother's forehead, looked her in the eye, and told her to go her way that she was healed. My mother walked off the platform all smiles and praising God. The long line continued.

My parents were notorious for sitting on the back row or second row from the back in church or the tent revivals. My dad had a fascination with the people, being new to Pentecostalism, and loved to watch the people dance in the spirit and receive the Holy Ghost. He sat in the back so he didn't miss anything. My mother returned to her seat on the other side of my father. My mother leaned in to him to whisper in his ear. I listened because I liked secrets.

"Feel Melvin, it is gone!" My mother stated lowly shielding her voice with her hand.

My father was reluctant to do so because they were out in public and the codes of what you could do in public back then were far different from now. He shook his head and said, "Later!"

"Everyone is watching the activity up front, Melvin. Feel . . . God has healed me. The egg of a lump in my breast is gone. I want you to see that it was an instant miracle."

He was still reluctant, so my mother picked his hand up and forced him to do so.

Red faced, he quickly felt and looked at my mother in total shock. The lump was totally gone. He took an ala natural look when he got home. There was no sign of a lump having ever existed.

There was a special miracle going on that night under Jack Cole's tent that probably those in attendance missed. My mother was not the only one healed of a lump or a tumor. There was also the man ahead of her. Both of their tumors disappeared immediately after prayer. Who knows how many other tumors were healed that night. Many were probably like my mother who couldn't speak openly of where their tumors were because of what was proper to talk about in public back then. God was in the tumor healing business that night and there is no telling how many others in that line were healed instantaneously. Jack Cole was a Holy Ghost filled healing evangelist, a tool of God.

My mother lived to be eighty-four, danced in the spirit, praised God, and never forgot her miracle. She lived to raise six children. She had a favorite song she sang the last few years of her life. It was from one of the old paperback hymnals sold at revivals back in the thirties and the forties.

"I will work, I will pray . . . in the vineyard . . . in the vineyard of the Lord."

My mother entered the vineyard when she was a child of eight or nine and stayed there till the day she crossed over.

CHAPTER EIGHT

The Hissing Demon

A young newcomer to the Pentecostal ranks named Brother Ed had just stepped into the Full Gospel Church office he was attending. The church had a lady pastor named Sister Lucy. Brother Ed could tell that she had a really serious look on her face as she hung up the phone.

"Come on Brother Ed. There is a woman that has been possessed of a demon and those at her place can't control her. We have to go now and cast it out." She stated grabbing her keys and a light jacket. She always wore navy blue, who knows why.

"What?" "He asked shaking in his boots?

Brother Ed was a good old Baptist boy newly called to the ministry and had been filled with the Pentecostal's Baptism in the Holy Ghost only recently.

Sister Lucy, a Holy Ghost and Fire woman minister and a firm believer in miracles, was always willing to put God and his miracle working power on the line. She wasn't afraid of anything and would tackle the Devil himself and never give it a second thought. Brother Ed on the other hand was new to the casting out demons thing and his knees were a little bit jelly.

"You heard me." She replied. Head for the car. You are driving. There is a battle to be fought with a demon from Hell and we are the ones on God's front line.

He obeyed and thought as he headed for the vehicle." God help me, I am in over my head this time!"

Brother Eddie had never prayed a demon out of anyone, came in contact with anyone having one, or knew anyone that had ever seen or heard one. He thought at first she was spoofing him. But when she started to pray in the Holy Ghost on the way to the address where they were headed, he was frightened thinking of what might happen if there was a demon bigger and stronger than him? He suddenly felt like he was treading deep water and needed to roll up his spiritual socks.

"Why are you taking me with you?" he asked as they were nearing their destination.

"You have more faith than anyone else in my church." Sister Lucy replied cool as a cucumber.

"I may have faith, but my knees are shaking. I have never seen or heard a demon before." He replied pulling the car into a parking space at their destination.

"Forget your knees. It isn't them that prays or has the power. You are God's chosen this morning to help me confront the Devil on his turf. There is war in the Spiritual Heaven's this morning. We are the soldiers chosen to go to war with our enemy. There is nothing to fear. Pull out your spiritual sword and prepare to do battle. We are the anointed army of God and the Devil is just his fallen angel." She stated climbing out of the front seat not waiting for him to circle the car and let her out. Brother Eddie was probably in his twenties and Sister Lucy was in her fifties.

"Wait for me . . . "he yelled as she wasted no time heading for the door to where the woman with the demon was said to be residing.

"Don't you think we should pray before we go in?" Brother Ed asked trying to buy himself some time. He admitted that he was frightened.

"I have done prayed on the way over. Come on, you are wasting God's time."

"Aren't you afraid of the devil or possibly his demon?" Brother Eddie asked following her thru the door which he didn't have time to open for her. She was on a mission and he was having trouble keeping up with her.

"I am a Holy Ghost filled woman. What do I have to fear? The devil can't enter a vessel that is full. I am a full vessel and so are you. You were baptized in the Holy Ghost last week weren't you?"

"Er . . . uh . . . yes . . . "He stated as she took down a long dark hallway of the building.

"God cast the Devil out of Heaven long ago and he has been looking for a way to get back in. He would like to try to enter Heaven riding in a human vehicle. Our cars are full. He is looking for a free ride in a junk vehicle. Those who don't have the Baptism are partially empty vessels and he is attempting to hi-jack one of them. We are going to cast him out of the human vehicle he has taken over. God cast him out of Heaven and we will cast him out again."

She said flying down the hall with Brother Eddie on her heels.

Brother Eddie muttered to himself as he followed her speedily. "God, you better help me. If that Devil is real, he may be bigger and meaner than me and I may be in big trouble." Fear gripped him even though he was hot on her heels.

"Why me . . . ?" He asked as they neared a door where there was a crowd gathered. "My knees are shaking.

"You are here by God's divine plan and you are to be the one who has my backside. No time to talk. It is time to battle. We are front line warriors." She said turning to glance briefly at him. "You watch my backside."

About that time, a screeching voice hissed from inside of the room where a crowd was gathered at its door. Sounds of things hitting the walls inside echoed. When Brother Eddie peeped over Sister Lucy's shoulder into the room where the hissing voice was, he saw a hundred pound petite teen female throwing grown men around like they were sofa pillows being tossed off a couch. No one could hold her down. Brother Eddie's knees then did some serious shaking and he went to doing some serious praying in the Holy Ghost. He was in over his head and he knew it.

From the girl's mouth inside of the room, a male voice was speaking. There was darkness in the girl's eyes that sparkled with flames of fire. She looked Sister Lucy directly in the eye and spoke.

"Sister Lucy, what in the Hell are you doing here?" the male voice asked in a hiss thru the girl. It was a demon that had entered her and was now speaking thru the teen girl. The personage of the petite, young, female was gone.

Christ cast out spirits and sent them into a group of swine. The teen girl was a swine type, a person not filled with the power of God. A loose demon with no body to walk the earth in had entered her vehicle days before according to those gathered at the door. She was a weak vessel, a swine, an easy target for a demon looking for housing.

Brother Eddie felt he was in over his head, but at the same time, he had faith in Sister Lucy and went to praying for God's shield around him and her. He did what he was told to do. He was there to pray and protect her backside. He wanted to be a steel shield of God behind her, but he felt like a crumpled piece of aluminum foil. As a piece of crumpled aluminum foil he did his best, gave his prayers their best, and stood behind her. That Devil continued to talk, hiss, and screech. Brother Eddie kept praying as he heard flames of Hell crackling in the demon's male voice. The crackling sounded like that coming off of wood logs that had been wet and stuck into a hot fire. There was steam and hissing.

Sister Lucy immediately stepped into the room and slapped her hand on the girl's head with no fear. The girl had been physically attacking everyone else, but she tried to cower and back up from Sister Lucy. Sister Lucy looked the demon in the eye and started speaking in tongues. As she prayed in the Holy Ghost, the demon began to get restless crying out in anguish and trying desperately to scoot away from her.

Brother Eddie eyed the girl that had been throwing around men bigger than him. He felt a little flustered thinking that the visibly possessed and agitated girl was going to eventually physically attack Sister Lucy and hurt her. He was a grown man and he was afraid. He continued to pray with beads of perspiration forming on his forehead and his deodorant had quit working.

Then Sister Lucy began to command the demon to do her bidding like it was a dog being trained to roll over and go back to where it came from. She demanded not flinching, "I rebuke you Satan in the Name of Jesus and command you to come out of her and return to Hell from whence you are trying to escape. Go back to Hell and never return to this girl. Come out of her now!" Then Sister Lucy began to speak in the Holy Ghost Mystery of Tongues and defied the demon from Hell staring it in the eye. She didn't flinch or break ranks.

Brother Eddie was praying, but he was also shaking in his shoes. He had never confronted a demon before. This one actually had the nerve to speak out loud to you. The deep male voice of the demon was raspy and sure of itself calling Sister Lucy by her name."

As Sister Lucy prayed in tongues, the girl suddenly became calm and the male voiced ceased. The student girl's voice returned and she asked Sister Lucy who she was and why she was there. The girl thought she had been asleep. The Demon left being no match for Sister Lucy and the miracle working Holy Ghost power of God that dwelt in her. Brother Eddie was also unharmed but possibly had wet undershorts. The girl had no memories of the casting out or sixty days prior. So, apparently the demon had entered her sixty days before the incident. The girl remembered going to a drunken party with her teen friends and that was the last she remembered.

Hang out where the devil or his demons are and you might just bring one home.

CHAPTER NINE

The Little War Path Indian

I have met and listened to a lot of Pentecostal ministers in my life, both famous and unknown. The one that sticks out in my memory is the pastor of a little church down in a country hollow that was known for an over abundance of possums. I don't recall the brother's name, but we will refer to him here as Brother Thurman. The event took place a good forty years ago possibly around 1970.

Brother Thurman couldn't read or write so his wife accompanied him and read the Bible for him. She would read a verse or two of scripture and then he spoke on what she read. They were an interesting couple. He was a short, skinny man and his wife was a fair size woman who had an extreme head of frizzy red hair. She would sit on the altar as she read for him and stay there till he was finished with his sermon. They were more interesting as a couple than eighty-five percent of the larger name Evangelists and their wives I have met. The couple had a large number of children of which at least five still lived at home at the time of this story.

Brother Thurman was a singer who picked a guitar. He and his family were well known in the area for singing one chorus having to do with him going to Heaven and looking for each member of his family and not immediately finding them there. When he was in tears finding that none of his family members had made it, he would give one last call before he went ahead and walked thru Heaven's gates alone. In the song, as the congregation pictured him on Heaven's shore, he would call out one of his family's names and then suddenly that individual would stand up in the church congregation and yell, "I am here, I am here, to answer my call." Then the individual just making it to Heaven's shore would go to shouting or rejoicing in the Holy Ghost.

Tears would roll down brother Thurman's face and he would move on and call his next child, wife, or family member's name to see if they had made it. He would strum his guitar and sing the following slowly.

"Oh daughter are you here . . . ?

"Oh daughter are you here . . .?

Are you here . . . Are you here . . . .

To answer your call . . . . ?"

The Holy Ghost would start to move people to compassion and tears as they saw the pastor in tears thinking each member of his family hadn't made it to Heaven.

He would sing it slow a second time strumming his guitar and hold the last line while he looked around in the congregation for them like he was on Heaven's shore. The crowd would always be quiet in anticipation because those of us who knew the minister knew what was coming.

Brother Thurman had one Holy Ghost filled daughter that was a shouter and when God moved on her you might as well get out of her way because she might shout and dance to the front altar and then run to the back door when the Holy Ghost had his way with her and then repeat it a couple of times.

As Brother Thurman sang slowly his last line ". . . to answer your call . . . ." His shouting daughter would rise to her feet and throw her hands in the air starting to tremble in the Holy Ghost.

In a slow voice matching her father's, she would sing, "I am here . . . I am here . . . to answer my call."

Then the Holy Ghost would hit her and she would begin to shake as she started to sing in an excited fast voice, "I just got to Heaven, to Heaven, to Heaven, I just got to Heaven to answer my call . . ."

Then the Holy Ghost would take control of her and she would dance all over Heaven, it being the aisles and front of the church. I can just imagine what going to Heaven with her would be like. Her Holy Ghost Heaven was a place of foot action.

Now she wasn't the only child of this couple. I think every kid they had was a shouter and a Holy Ghost Dancer.

When the first one had calmed a little and was standing in the middle of the church aisle trembling with hands in the air and oblivious to the crowd, he would sing the call again. Once more a child or family member would stand and answer their call.

On the night I was there, the second called was a high school aged boy who stood and raised his arms into the air and closed his eyes and began to sing the slow response, "I am here . . . I am here . . . to answer my call."

43

The boy was a crier and tears started running down his face and his voice choked as he reached the end of the slow response. Then he started singing slowly and softly, "I just got to heaven, to heaven, to heaven." Then he would pause a moment wiping tears on the back of his one hand and then started speeding up his singing of the final part of 'I just got to Heaven' repeating the chorus a couple of times as fast as he could belt it out. Then with eyes full of tears and his hands extended as far into the air as he could reach, he would start to speak in tongues and his body would start to shake and tremble. He was a Holy Ghost language man. He gave a message in tongues as well as then interpreted it. Those in the congregation shivered in the Holy Ghost and the church was about to explode.

When calm once more settled, Brother Thurman then called one of his younger daughter's names. "Are you here . . . are you here . . . to answer your call?"

This time a preteen girl stood and raised her hands to heaven. She was about eleven and the spitting image of her mother with a full head of red frizzy curly hair that was pulled up in a wild pony tail.

This child stepped out into the middle of the center aisle as she answered her call.

"I am here . . . I am here . . . to answer my call." Then the congregation started to sing with her, "I just got to Heaven, to Heaven, to Heaven. I just got to Heaven to answer my call."

The congregation was ready for their call. They were trembling and sitting on the edge of their seats.

As the congregation was helping the pre-teen sing the last of her 'I just got to Heaven', you could see her bend one knee under the anointing of the Holy Ghost. Then she started to dance in a circle spinning under the power of the Holy Ghost. She had her hands straight out to the sides and as she danced and shouted spinning, her feet were doing a step that only God could have put in them. She repetitively twirled in a circle like a child's toy top. When she quit spinning, she was drunk in the Holy Ghost and just stood lost in the center of the aisle praising God and rocking back and forth.

A couple of more calls went out with the preacher's wife answering and shouting all over the front of the church. Then another child in his teens was called who was also a shouter. Then there was only one child left, a little boy about six years old.

Brother Thurman began his last call, "Oh Billy, are you here? Are you here . . . are you here . . . to answer your call."

Immediately, the little boy climbed up on the pew he was sitting on and everyone moved off of it. He stood facing his father grinning.

Billy began to sing slowly in his child's voice "I am here . . . I am here . . . to answer my call."

The congregation sang the now familiar 'I just got to Heaven' for him. He couldn't contain his excitement. He started to move his legs and dance like he was an Indian on the war path. He put one hand over his mouth and started clapping it making that mouth noise Indians make while dancing around campfires. Then the Holy Ghost got a hold of Billy and he had one major, Holy Ghost, war path, pew dancing moment. Up and down the pew he war danced with his eyes closed, never falling off.

Then, Brother Thurman called the whole congregation to answer their call as a group. That church was alive and I have never seen so many manifestations of God and the Holy Ghost at one time in one place.

Needless to say, the preacher didn't get to speak that night. Just before closing in prayer, the pastor said one last thing as everyone was sitting in the pews calming down.

"You want to watch out for that little Indian. He knows how to dance and make war on that old enemy, the Devil."

CHAPTER TEN

The Holy Ghost Deflates an Ego

Back in the late 1960's, I was attending a very tiny Full Gospel Church that was held in a tiny rock house that had been reconfigured into a tiny church. The building was barely twenty-four feet square and had no room for Sunday school rooms or amenities. If you needed to use restroom facilities, you had to go and ask a neighbor of the church to use theirs or go down to a service station which was about a quarter of a mile away. The inside walls of the tiny structure had been removed and every inch of space was used for seating. There were five rows of folding chairs with a center aisle. Up front, there was barely room for an altar and a handmade speaker's stand. Behind the podium, there was barely room for the minister to stand and preach. To the right of the podium, flat against the right wall, set one slat back pew where the minister set with whoever else might be helping with the service for the evening. On the other side of the podium was a huge upright piano. It was placed in such a fashion that the pianist always sat with his back to the congregation.

The little down home, improvised, church structure was what the group could afford. The center walls of the tiny house had been removed and a couple of iron posts had been put in to support the overhead beam that would have been held up by a wall. The metal posts you just dealt with and walked around them. There was no decorator hired to make the inside of the chapel appealing. It was like a plain Jane hand me down dress. Whatever was donated was used and that included mismatched folding chairs, a hand built podium, an altar from scrap boards, an antique upright piano, and one slat back pew for the minister to sit on. There was no fancy sound system. It wasn't needed in a space that is the size of some living rooms in houses built today. It was tiny, cozy, mismatched in décor, and filled every service night to overflowing. The Holy Ghost isn't in to decorating or size. He is into people expecting a visitation.

A plush wingback chair for the minister to sit in will not bring the power of God down. A brand new baby grand piano will not bring the power of God down. A designer worn suit will not bring the power of God down. A red plush carpet down the center aisle of a church will not bring the power of God down. Thousands of dollars spent on plush padded pews will not bring the power of God down. The Holy Ghost power of God comes down to hearts that are willing to seek him. He could be sitting in the tiniest of church structures where material things are not seen as God's prosperity. Many men sit on expensive pews in expensive structures who have never experienced the infilling of the Holy Ghost because there is no one preaching it and willing to tarry with those beyond service times for them to receive. Men want God on a pre-planned time schedule. God is colorful spontaneity moving when he wants, not when we want. It is us that must tarry and wait on him, not him with us.

Waiting on God was the agenda of the tiny church that I am writing about. They were there to meet and receive something from God; not to hold to any form or planned services. They were open to whatever God and the Holy Ghost wished to do in each service even if it meant getting out at one- thirty on Sunday instead of twelve.

The pianist had the worst seat in that little church. He had to sit on the piano bench during service and had to twist around on it during service to see what was happening. Every seat in the tiny church was always filled and when the pianist was finished playing, he was forced to remain on his bench at the piano. Brother Dan, the Pianist, was gracious and never complained.

Brother Dan was a young man, possibly twenty one or twenty two. He was single, had a flair for fashion, as well as playing the piano hot when the Holy Ghost started falling. There wasn't a key he couldn't play in, even though he played by ear or by his gift given him by the Holy Ghost. He didn't play the piano before receiving the Holy Ghost. He could play anything on the church's Victorian piano equal to any professional musician of that day. He was young, extremely handsome, loveable in spirit, and Holy Ghost gifted.

On one particular night back then, the Holy Ghost had made his presence known during song service. People had flooded the altar and the Holy Ghost had his way in many forms. There had been tongues and interpretation, shouting, praises, and the gifts of the spirit demonstrated. People danced in the spirit and raised their hands to Heaven in tears and praise. The Holy Ghost was present and swept over the congregation and in and out of those who had tarried for the Baptism.

Brother Dan was an easy going fellow who was friendly, blushed easily, and was liked by everyone. He was also flashy in his dress and expressions of words. Several of the younger women in the church were interested in him and he was living the good life as a single Pentecostal man. He was hot as the girls would say today. In the Pentecostal ranks, he was considered quite a holy man as well as a hunk. The word hunk wasn't used back then, but it fits now in my thinking. He was an extremely handsome dashing figure. He had movie star quality and could have easily been a part of a professional, famous singing or gospel music group somewhere.

On the particular night I am writing about, Brother Dan had on a black suit that was fresh back from the cleaners and he looked really sharp. He had on a white shirt with a bright red necktie .On his shirt cuffs he wore ruby cufflinks that were flashing as he played. On a finger on his right hand he wore a huge man's ring with a ruby set in it. A red man's handkerchief was precisely placed in his suit jacket pocket. He looked nice and probably was a little prideful in how he looked. Brother Dan was the eye candy for the evening to those who perhaps weren't as spiritual as the others and were peepers like me.

Brother Dan sat with his back to us playing the piano hot. The song service was in full swing. Those who were not getting in with God and moving in the Holy Ghost were staring at the back of the church star Brother Dan. I was nineteen and single. I will have to admit that I was guilty of looking him over a little bit. What young woman hasn't looked at a handsome man and dreamed of a Holy Ghost Knight in shining armor. I admit that I was looking him over that night. However, Brother Dan would not be mine. A friend of mine won the heart of Bro. Dan. She was considered to be quite homely to the point of being just plain out ugly. She definitely had no flash or fashion sense of her own. However, she had something we didn't have. She knew how to tarry at the altar for what she wanted and she went every church service and prayed in the Holy Ghost asking God for the flashy Brother Dan.

There was no preaching the night I am writing about. The Holy Ghost swept thru the congregation having his way. Bro. Dan played and sang between the Gifts of the God that were manifesting. The pastor ministered using the Word of Knowledge to members of his congregation. There were tongues and interpretations. God's will and the Holy Ghost's moving didn't fit a pre-made plan or program.

Service was coming to close and it was about ten o'clock at night. The last song was being played and the service winding down when a four year old boy got away from his mother and sprinted for the piano bench and climbed up on it next to Brother Dan. Brother Dan was gracious and just let him sit there knowing that service was almost over. Brother Dan was still facing away from the congregation. The boy, a stranger to the church, sat on the piano bench facing the congregation with his back to the piano. Brother Dan gave him a quick grin and then did a last run on the piano keys ending the last song with a flourish. He then turned his shoulders so he could smile and give the congregation a final wave for the evening. He was pleased with his part of the service and you could see on his face that he was proud of himself and probably about how he looked for the evening.

Just as Brother Dan turned his shoulders all smiles and raised his arm to give his little showmanship wave to the people, the church suddenly got so still that you could have heard a pin drop or a fly buzz. Just as that quiet moment and Brother Dan had everyone's attention, the little boy let one of the loudest, biggest, longest, echoing winds I have ever heard in my life. It seemed to vibrate off the wooden piano bench and then off the walls. I had no trouble hearing it on the back row where I was sitting with my friends.

Everyone's mouth dropped open including the mother of the child whom we never saw again. Brother Dan instantly turned the most brilliant shade of red. He embarrassed really easy. Then he looked down at the little boy who looked up at him.

The little kid raised his hand and pointed his finger at Brother Dan saying, "He did it!"

Then the little boy slapped his hand over his mouth laughing, jumped off the piano bench, and ran to his mother.

You could tell by Brother Dan's face that he was totally humiliated. He was unable to speak. He couldn't defend himself and say he didn't do it and look like an egotistical fool. He couldn't alienate the mother by insinuating the kid was a liar denying it. The congregation was small and every member needed. All he could do was blush and then drop his head. The congregation roared with laughter and then got up and went home.

The Holy Ghost moved that night and took Brother Dan's pride as the last event of the service. I cannot recall him wearing that black suit and red accessories after that. He dressed down blending in with the members of the congregation. If it hadn't been for the fact that he was related to the pastor, I doubt if he would have ever returned to play again. He was one ego deflated Holy Ghost man.

On that same night, one of my friends received the Baptism of the Holy Ghost with the evidence of speaking in tongues. I received an eye full of a handsome man. In the long run, my eyeing Brother Dan gained me nothing in my walk with God. However, I looked and the above is what I saw. God was calling me to be a writer, but I just didn't see it at that point. The Holy Ghost wanted my eyes open. At the time, I didn't realize that I would one day in the future write about the Holy Ghost and different services that I peeped at.

"Let him . . . have eyes to see and ears to hear, (I am adding) and a pen to write!"

Today, I am a writer and tell of the things my eyes have seen. I still peep in services, however, not at flashy piano players. I like to watch people dance in the spirit when the Holy Ghost is moving on them. I find happy feet fascinating.

CHAPTER ELEVEN

Singing in the Holy Ghost

In my years as a Pentecostal woman, I have heard a lot of references made to people being anointed as they sang or presented the special music for a service. They were referred to as having been anointed by or feeling the Holy Ghost as they sang.

There is a difference between singing in the Holy Ghost and someone feeling the spirit or Holy Ghost as they sing.

Someone who presents their hymn or special music in their natural voice feels the spirit or Holy Ghost as they sing. They have a feeling experience. Singing in the Holy Ghost is singing in tongues.

I have heard a lot of beautiful hymns sung and the anointing of God pass over the singer in a feeling. However, I have also heard Holy Ghost filled men and women sing songs of Heaven which are not earth songs. Singing in the Holy Ghost or unknown tongues has a sound and rhythm all its own, just as a man speaking in tongues is different. Natural voice singers are feeling the spirit singers. Holy Ghost singers are tongue singers. There is a difference. Natural singers have the ball bat feeling experience as they sing. Holy Ghost Singers have the Holy Ghost coming out from within them singing in unknown tongues. There is a difference between having a spirit pass over your head and you feel it and one that lives within you and manifests from there. Singing in the Holy Ghost in tongues is a higher experience.

I think Pentecostal people sell themselves short and don't seek the fullness of God which includes the singers of the church tarrying till the Holy Ghost sings thru them in tongues. A lot of cute people get behind the pulpit and sing cute songs, however, how many times have you heard a singer who has tarried till he is able to get up and sing in the Holy Ghost in tongues? Someone singing with the spirit passing over them making them feel good is a second best experience. The power in the Holy Ghost for a singer is to be able to sing in tongues. Better yet is for a singer in tongues then to be able to sing the interpretation of the song he has just sung. There is a fuller experience in the Holy Ghost that the Pentecostals are missing out on. That is the reason the churches are dying off and getting cold. The tarrying for the fullness of God and the Holy Ghost and its evidence of speaking in tongues has been abandoned.

About the year of 1970, I just happened to accompany a person to hear a visiting evangelist from Arizona to where I was living at the time. There wasn't a big turn out and the evangelist and his wife were at the altar praying for services. After services, his wife returned to the altar to pray for God's will as whether to continue the revival where no one was attending, or to move on to a new location.

The men in attendance also fell into the altar to pray. The men all had an agenda for their prayers and were having at it beseeching God for an answer in their natural voices. I heard a lot of verbal prayers from the men, but none of them were praying in the Holy Ghost or tongues.

I was young at the time, in my twenties, and I liked to peek from my own prayers and see what was going on. Now, I know the reason for my curiosity. I needed to observe to be able to write about the Holy Ghost in the future.

The wife of the evangelist didn't seem to have an agenda. She spoke no earthly words as she began to pray. Being the only woman at the altar, she knelt at a far end by herself. Instead of praying in natural words, she began to speak in tongues and then began to sing in tongues. Her voice quivered high and then low and then ran like a deer across a landscape. Out of her mouth flowed unknown tongues in the form of music. Whatever it was that she was singing had to be before the thrown of God because it was the most beautiful sounds I have ever heard. There was no recognizable tune that might fit one of Earth church hymns or popular Christian songs of the time. Each line of the tongues was different and had its own rhythm and movement from her mouth. The flittering flight of a butterfly is a beautiful thing. The words coming from her mouth were taking flight like hundreds of little wings and each was a quiver, a sound, a word in an unknown language.

I have never heard anything like it before or since. It wasn't just a word or two in tongues. It was a complete song. The men were praying and feeling the Holy Ghost, but she was singing in the Holy Ghost. The men were giving lip service. She was letting the Holy Ghost work and serve thru her.

If you are a singer, ask God to fill your mouth with the Song of Heaven. Anyone can sing Earth's hymns. The power is in Heaven's songs sung in the Holy Ghost. Seek it just like you did when you sought the Holy Ghost with the evidence of Speaking in tongues. Don't settle for being second best. The natural voice is second best. Let the wings of Heaven, Holy Ghost tongues, use your voice. That is where your power as a singer lies.

Don't be happy singing Earth words where you just feel the Holy Ghost moving on you. Let the Holy Ghost have your mouth and be a vessel thru which he sings. Don't settle for just a feeling as you sing experience.

CHAPTER TWELVE

Thank You for the Miracle That is on the Way

Back in the early 1990s I was traveling south going thru a little town in a mountainous region. I had a friend who was a truck driver and I was making a short trip with him just for the heck of it with no particular agenda in mind. It was Sunday, and for some odd reason, he was forced by his dispatcher to make a delivery in small country town on a Sunday. As a rule, loads aren't usually accepted on Sundays, especially in a small Bible belt town. His plan was to unload, make a u-t urn, and then head back out of the mountains to the interstate and return where we started and have supper in a truck stop. I was then and still am a writer. At the time, I was thinking of writing a book of fiction about a trucker. The ride with him was a learning experience and research, or so I thought.

We were passing thru one small town headed for the next one down. We had to stop at a four way stop and it seemed the cars were stalled for some reason slowing us down. Looking ahead, I spotted a tiny Pentecostal church in a storefront building. It was pretty unassuming with a plain white paper church sign hung with tape in the window and a simple red cross hung above the doorway. Someone in the congregation had probably made both because they couldn't afford a professional sign. For some reason, I wanted to get off that truck and stay for service which really wasn't possible. My friend was on a tight schedule and he definitely wasn't Pentecostal, much less a practicing Christian of any sort. I just had an overwhelming need to get out and go to that service.

"Mack, let me out in front of that little storefront after we pull thru the four way stop. I think I will attend service and you can pick me up after you deliver and make your turn around."

"That could be hours, Jo. I have no guarantee how fast I will get unloaded."

"It doesn't matter. I will sit on that retaining wall on the outside and wait for you. I just really don't want to sit in a manufacturer's parking lot all morning."

"Okay, but I can't promise how quick I will get back here for you. You could be here all day."

"That is alright. I see a convenience store about two blocks down. I can grab myself a snack and a drink there if necessary. The weather is beautiful and I could use a little sun and stretch my legs a little bit."

It was very evident that the little town was into Sunday shut down. The only thing open was the little storefront church and the convenience store.

"This is against my better judgment, Jo. Some small town jerk of a cop could give you grief thinking you are homeless or something."

"I will be fine. Just let me out."

So, my friend, a truck driver let me out.

I glanced at my watch. it was about three minutes till eleven. Sunday school was sure to be over and morning worship about to begin. After getting out, I knew from the sign on the front window that services would start in a minute or so. I quickly opened the single storefront church door and stepped inside taking a seat in the third row from the front. There were only four rows of folding chairs. I was shocked to see almost no one in attendance. There were only seven people and they were all on their knees in the front around the altar and praying for what I thought was the service. I sat down quietly so as not to disturb.

I heard a tall looking black man at the altar moan and say, "God send us a miracle! God send us a miracle. God send us a miracle!"

You could tell from the sound of his voice that there was a desperate need. I assumed someone in their tiny church had to be in need of healing and whoever it was could possibly be at death's door. I sat respectfully with my head hung low and continued to look about the tiny storefront chapel. The speaker's stand was handmade from rough boards and everything in there seemed to have an eclectic thrown together look with nothing matching. They were a poor church ministering to poor people, I told myself.

When the black man, that I assumed was the minister, stopped groaning and asking for a miracle in simple words, a Hispanic woman on her knees down a little ways from him started to repeat his request in the same simple words.

"Send us a Miracle, God. We need a miracle. Send us a miracle!" She prayed as tears rolled down her cheeks.

Since she was in tears, I assumed it was probably someone in her family that was very ill and maybe at death's door. I continued to bow my head and glance about the little church that was set up in a dilapidated storefront building that didn't look like it had been painted in twenty years.

There were three young guys in their twenties at the altar that didn't look like the black man or the Hispanic woman. However, they had raven black hair and looked Hispanic. They were also praying the same prayer.

"Send us a miracle, God"

"We need a miracle, God."

"We need a miracle today, God"

There was one odd individual at the altar. An elderly white headed woman was knelt at the far end of the altar. She had her head buried in her arms praying. Her words were a little different.

"Thank you for the miracle, God. Thank you for our miracle, God. Thank you for our miracle."

Older, seasoned members of the Pentecostal ranks know to thank God for their miracle that is on the way. They pray with wisdom in their prayers. I could tell she was sincere in her thanking God just as the others were sincere in their asking. Whoever was dying had to be hanging on by a thread in my mind."

I kept my head down and at about one minute after eleven the three rose and each took their place. Service started with the black man leading the song service. The Hispanic woman walked back offering a quick greeting handshake and then took her place up front.

The man leading the service proceeded to call out a number in their hymnal for everyone to turn to. I didn't see a hymnal in front of me or on the bench. The Hispanic woman quickly walked to my row and handed me hers. Then, everyone paired up and I could see that the church only had four hymnals and they were all sharing them. I felt really guilty having one all to myself.

Apparently, the congregation was a mixed one with the majority of the seven or so there being Spanish. I heard someone slip in behind me and take a quick seat possibly making the congregation count for the morning, seven to eight people. I didn't look back. I wonder now, if it wasn't possibly Christ or the Holy Ghost that entered and took a seat for the morning.

No mention was made of who the congregation had been praying at the altar for. Service was held according to their traditions. I didn't have any cash on me when the offering plate came around, so I passed it on. When riding on a truck, you don't carry cash on you in case you get robbed or mugged in a truck stop somewhere. However, I had a blank check in my pocket for an emergency should I need it. When the offering plate passed, I did not consider the check or remember it. Had I done so, I might have made it out for five or ten and placed it in the plate. In my pocket was a credit card to make purchases from the convenience store after service if needed. The offering plate went by and after a special song by the older woman who had been at the altar with her head buried in her arms, the pastor got up to speak. It wasn't the black man as I had expected. The pastor was the Hispanic woman who had shaken my hand. She preached Hell Hot and Holiness absolute, take it or leave it. I squirmed a little because I wasn't exactly sitting there in my Sunday best. I told myself to not worry about it, that I had on my best for the morning, and it was what it was.

I tuned part of her sermon out as I glanced around the little building realizing how they were really struggling. They were singing out of a handful of hymnals, sitting in dented worn out metal folding chairs, and were kneeling to pray on rough unpainted wooden floors.

It was at that point that I really felt that I should try to help them in some way. I had just got my income tax back and it was a very large amount. So, remembering the blank check in my pocket, I pulled it out and using an ink pen that was loose in the hymnal holder in front of me, I wrote out a check for seven hundred dollars and had it ready to hand to the church pastor as I exited services. I decided to just hand her the check and exit quickly hoping that my friend's turn around in the truck would be a quick one. It was about twelve- thirty and the service had lasted a little longer than I had anticipated because the minister had a lot to say and she laid it on her congregation. I didn't have a clue what they had been up to. There was only about seven or so of them. They all seemed sincere in their prayers and they were dressed in holiness attire with long sleeves and high necks, etc. I was sure that whatever their sin was, it couldn't have been too bad.

After asking if anyone needed prayer and then giving an altar call, the pastor closed service. I quietly rose, waited till the pastor took position at the back door to bid the members of her congregation farewell, and got in the short line. I wanted to exit quickly. Finally, it came my turn.

As she reached out her hand to shake, I handed her the check instead and told her I thought I would like to help them out a bit and to use the money however she felt would best serve the interest of the church. She opened the check. I had folded it to prevent anyone from seeing how much it was. She gasped, grabbed her heart, and looked at me with a solemn shocked look. I could tell that she was at a loss for words.

"You will have to write the church's name in because I don't know what you are called." I stated trying to break the ice. She was in shock and not speaking.

Regaining her composure, she grabbed my hand with the one not holding the check, shook and squeezed my hand hard not letting go. After biting her lip to hold back tears, she spoke.

"If it wasn't for the fact that you have handed me a check and I can read your name and address on it, I would believe you are an angel sent to us from God. Before service, we were all on our knees praying for a major financial miracle. We don't have the rent for this building. We were going to have to close our doors today and move out if a miracle didn't come by noon. We owe two month's rent of three hundred and fifty dollars each. The landlord told us to move out after service today if we didn't give him a full seven hundred dollars."

I grinned, shook her hand, and excused myself. I didn't have time to wait around and converse with her. I could see my friend pulled along the curb on the opposite side of the street waiting for me.

My opinion is that God can make angels or miracle workers out of people, if he wants.

Climbing up in the semi-truck, I asked my friend, "Why are you back so soon?"

"The strangest thing happened. I went down there. Instead of my having to wait to unload, they took my trailer from me and had me back up under this pre-loaded one going back the direction we just came from. I basically did a quick turn around and here I am. I have been sitting here about three or four minutes.

I didn't have to sit on a retainer wall and wait. God sent his chariot of fire for me. My friend made the wheels of his big rig hum leaving the mountain area where we were. He didn't have a clue that he was part of a God destined Holy Ghost miracle. He had no interest in religion and would turn on the CB or radio if you started referring to the subject. My trucker friend that year jumped from making thirty-five thousand dollars for the year to sixty-four thousand. If he hadn't stopped and let me out in front of that storefront when God wanted me out, I just imagine he might have went off a mountain somewhere and possibly made nothing for the next year. You don't mess with God or who he has chosen to deliver a miracle.

A week later, I ended up in Springfield, Missouri where there is a gospel publisher that prints hymnals in various languages. I purchased a box of Hymnals in Spanish and sent them to the tiny storefront church in the mountain town where I had been the previous week.

That small Spanish speaking congregation prayed! God heard and sent me! The strange thing was; God let me hear all of them praying in English. The pastor was a Spanish speaking woman.

The Holy Ghost moves speaking thru men in unknown tongues. I had an experience just the opposite. The Holy Ghost gave me ears to understand a language I did not speak. They prayed in Spanish, I heard in English.

It has been twenty some years and I am sure that the members of that small congregation have moved on to bigger and better things in God and the church pastor possibly deceased. She was an old Hispanic woman back then. If she were alive now, she would have to be over a hundred years old.

CHAPTER THIRTEEN

My Two Healings

I personally, as the writer of this book of Holy Ghost stories, have had two healings as the direct result of a Pentecostal minister praying in the Holy Ghost for me.

When I was about five, around the year of 1950, I had the whooping cough. It was a miserable, red face turning, hacking cough. When the cough hit you, you would cough maybe ten times in a row violently only to catch your breath and then do it again over and over. Once the cough started, it was like a never ending freight train of coughs. I was standing on our enclosed back porch with my mother. The enclosed porch was our laundry room and a wringer washer resided there. A knock sounded at the back porch door and my mother answered it. The visitor was my Uncle Bill whose story is told earlier in this book. He had come to speak with my mother about cutting his hair. My mother, who was his sister, often cut the hair of the men in the family to save them money. My mother was not a barber, etc. She just did her best to help her family who were all poor. Hair cuts for my brothers and my Uncle Bill were a common place occurrence. My father however, always went to the Barber Shop. He said my mother gave bowl cuts and he was a crew cut man.

My mother opened the door and was quite happy to see Uncle Bill and immediately explained to him that I had the whooping cough and she was concerned that something might happen to me because my coughing was so violent. I can remember the violent coughing and an attack of it as Uncle Bill and my mother were speaking.

"Bill, I want you to pray for her." My mother stated as he stepped onto the back porch and closed the door. Uncle Bill was a huge tall man and he had to stoop way down to deal with me. He put his huge hands on each side of my tiny child's face and began to speak in tongues. Then in his natural voice he prayed asking God to deliver me. After he left, I never coughed again with the whooping cough. God answered my uncle's prayers. I got healed and he got a haircut."

"Why would God heal me and not another child with the same affliction in the same city? In my thinking, God knew that one day I would be writing this book and sharing my Holy Ghost Pentecostal background. This is a testimony to the power of God and a man who let the Holy Ghost pray thru him. I have no idea what he said in tongues. Whatever it was, God heard and I was healed."

When I was a senior in high school, I had another affliction hit me. One Friday afternoon in high school, my neck started drawing and my head tipped to one side. I was unable to straighten it and there was pain in trying to do so. I lay down for most of the weekend because of my bent head position. On the third day, my cousin Lester came from Kansas City for a visit. He was a Holy Ghost filled Pentecostal and also a firm believer in prayer. He saw himself as a minister, an evangelist. My mother asked him to pray for me. He immediately did and in tongues. When I lay back down immediately afterwards, my neck snapped back into position and the pain in the muscles was gone. A Holy Ghost man prayed in tongues and a miracle happened. My head before prayer was almost lying on my shoulder.

My family was Pentecostal and as a rule, did not run to the doctor. They prayed first. The year of my healing was 1963. My Holy Ghost filled cousin prayed for me letting the Holy Ghost speak thru him in tongues just as Uncle Bill had when I was afflicted with the whooping cough.

CHAPTER FOURTEEN

Send Down the Reindeer, Lord

It was about 1950 when my parents attended a city wide revival crusade in the Shrine Mosque of Springfield, Missouri. I don't remember who the evangelist for the crusade was, but I do remember the place was packed. The evangelist had to of been a major well know evangelist because there was at least a thousand people there.

I was five or so at the time. My little brother was three or so and my older brother was eight possibly. My little brother was just barely big enough to sing and walk in and out of the crusade without having to be carried.

My baby brother was a little tow headed boy with lily white skin. I was a skinny little girl with long hair. My brother Ralph was a live wire who played hard but behaved in church. Our father would have tanned our backsides when we got home if we didn't. It didn't take but one tanning of our hides to make us behaved when we were in public. We were just an ordinary family, except that my parents were Holy Ghost filled and walked the straight and narrow.

At the crusade, I remember a male song leader getting up and singing the following lines which was a chorus:

"Send down the rain Lord - Send down the rain Lord

. . . Send down the latter rain.

Send down the rain Lord – Send down the rain Lord

. . . Send down the latter rain."

The chorus was repeated over and over with the multitude of crusade attendees joining in with the song leader singing before the preaching.

My baby brother who was about four was sitting between me and my older brother Ralph. My mother had purposely chosen to seat my four year old brother between us in case the Holy Ghost started to move. If my mother or dad got happy, as they called it back then in the Pentecostal ranks, my brother and I had our four year old brother secure between us. I was told to keep an eye on him as well as was my brother Ralph. That was common in big families back then. The older siblings watched out for the younger.

I assume now that it was Christmas time, possibly December due to a song my little four year old brother sang that night. Before I go on with my story, let me tell you that my family didn't teach us that there was a Santa Claus, Easter Bunny, or a tooth fairy. There was Christ and the Holy Ghost and that was who we heard about. However, my four year old brother was big into reindeer for some reason. He didn't hear about reindeer in our house, so he could have picked it up from one of the aunts, uncles, or cousins who weren't dyed in the wool Pentecostal.

I don't know whether my little brother had a head cold possibly or had a slight hearing problem the night of the crusade. He heard the Latter Rain chorus differently from us and sang at the top of his lungs along with the crowd his version.

"Send down the reindeer Lord - Send down the reindeer Lord

. . . Send down the late reindeer.

Send down the reindeer Lord - Send down the reindeer Lord

. . . Send down the late reindeer."

My brother Ralph and I were amused and didn't tell him any difference. He was singing with all of his little heart a song of praise and we just let him sing it how he was hearing it. On the way home, he sang it in the car like it was the best song that he had ever heard. My parents were even a little amused, although they didn't embrace the teaching of Santa and his Reindeer.

I have often wondered what voice my little brother was hearing that night. He was visibly into the song service and didn't know he was singing something the others weren't. He got just as much of a blessing out of his version as did the Pentecostal Latter Rain people did singing and praising God with their version. Perhaps God and the Holy Ghost were amused on that night over sixty years ago.

The next day was Monday and my mother's laundry day. She always washed the first day of the week. My parents were predictable people who always followed budgets and did the same things at the same time. We never had dirty clothes because my mother had a routine and she stuck with it. We had a full porch that ran across the back of our house. Dad closed it in and made my mother a laundry room out of it. A wringer washer and a set of galvanized metal tubs where she rinsed the clothes dominated the porch. There were no dryers back in that day so my mother , like everyone else, hung her clothes out on the line to dry twelve months a year.

We lived in the city and there were houses all around us. We lived in an established housing section that had been there for some time. It was not countryside. We were center city as they say now.

On that particular morning after the Latter Rain crusade, my mother took a basket of freshly washed wet clothes outside and was pinning them on the line in the cold. My little brother stood in the open doorway of the porch watching her. She was hurrying because it was winter and she wanted to get back inside to warm herself. My mother was using peg clothespins because she didn't have the spring ones yet at that time. She would put two or three peg- heads in her mouth and proceed down the line to speed up the clothes hanging process.

As she pinned dad's last wet shirt on the line, she glanced up at the row of houses behind her across the alley and saw a deer with one of the biggest racks of antlers she had ever seen run between two houses there and then bound across the alley heading for her at the clothes line. She screamed, ran, and barely stepped into the back porch door when the monster buck ran within inches of her and then around our house and disappeared. My little brother was standing in the door watching and grinning. He then once more went to singing, Send down the reindeer, Lord."

Does God hear children? My little four year old brother was quite amused with the big late reindeer that God sent down to chase his mother into the house.

Children have their own take on God. They pray and believe for things we see as totally unimportant. I am sure that God is amused at times and answers children according to how they see things .My brother wanted blessed with a reindeer and he got one.

May the Holy Ghost have his way with your small children and God be amused and answer their Reindeer Prayers!

CHAPTER FIFTEEN

The Latter Rain and the Baptism in Fire

When I was twenty or twenty-two, I attended a revival meeting where a woman evangelist was speaking. She was very popular in the area where I lived and held a revival every couple of weeks somewhere in the area. God was blessing her ministry and people were being baptized in the Holy Ghost and healed. She was an unusual looking woman who had a split between her two front buck teeth that kept your attention. I wouldn't say she was a pretty woman, except in the Holy Ghost. When she prayed in tongues in the Holy Ghost, she took on an aura that gave her the appearance of being angelic. If there was a miracle happening in the area, it was taking place in one of her revivals.

Thinking back, I realize that she was on a friendship basis with her Holy Ghost. He wasn't some mysterious force or being that just happened to float over her now and then. She let her friend speak thru her in tongues and did what he said to do, no questions asked. Looking back, I realize that the male ministers in the same area were happy with just asking God to sweep over their congregations during service times. They didn't have the Holy Ghost dwelling in them seven days a week. They had a feeling relationship with the Holy Ghost. The men were calling on a God and a Holy Ghost that were dwelling in a far off sky somewhere to come down and use a bat and hit their people and them over the head with blessings. Sister Ette was calling on the Holy Ghost that lived within her to do miracles using her hands as tools. She wasn't calling on a far off Holy Ghost who lived in the sky somewhere. There is a difference. Knowing you have the power and the Holy Ghost within is different than calling on the Spirit of God to come from some mysterious far off place and pass over you and your congregation.

There are two groups of Pentecostals.

1. Number one is the ones that speak in tongues and the Holy Ghost

resides within them seven days a week. He is not a spirit that resides some-where far off in the sky somewhere. This group tarries at the altar till they have the Holy Ghost who speaks in tongues thru their mouth. They know where the Holy Ghost resides and it is within them. They call the Holy Ghost the Holy Ghost. They have a knowing the Holy Ghost is in them experience.

2. Number two is the ones that feel a Holy Spirit passing over them. They have a feeling experience and speak of the Spirit of God sweeping over their congregation. Their Holy Spirit or Holy Ghost lives in a far off place and oc-casionally passes over. They have strictly a feeling experience.

Sister Ette was a Holy Ghost within Pentecostal. The Holy Ghost resided in her and not in the far off sky somewhere. She didn't need a Holy Spirit to come down, sweep over her, and slap her on the head once in a while to get her attention. She was on a first name basis with him and he lived within her.

I would say that ninety-five percent of the feeling Pentecostals have never tarried at the altar for the indwelling experience. Also, they have not tarried asking God and the Holy Ghost whether it is okay to do this or that, wear this or that, and how to live their lives according to God's will not theirs. God is a Holy God and the FEELING THE SPIRIT PENTECOSTALS don't seem to have conviction on them for the need to change their lives and walk according to God's standards. God does have standards. God is holy. The Holy Ghost is holy. Neither will dwell in an unclean vessel. However, they might pass over and hit you upside the head with a feeling experience trying to get your attention now and then.

Sister Ette was half hated by the male ministers of the Pentecostal ranks. Men get jealous of those displaying what they do not have. Men hate even worse a woman who is displaying what they do not have. It didn't matter what the male ministers thought, she was the vessel that the Holy Ghost was working thru performing miracles. You have heard the old saying, PUT UP OR SHUT UP? Sister Ette was able to put up. The male ministers were not.

I knew a woman in the church named Gwen. She was new to Pentecos-talism and had been tarrying for several nights to be filled with the Holy Ghost. She was not an educated woman. Her husband trimmed trees for a living. She had two sons who were in their teens and she was a stay at home mother and housewife. She was an ordinary woman with possibly a tenth grade education. I knew her casually in the church because she was quite a bit older than me and we just had different friends. I hung out with those in the church who were my age. As I said before, I was twenty-two. She was at least thirty-five or forty and had her set of older women that she was friends with. I had no children and she had teenage children. Our worlds and lives were just different.

After several nights of tarrying, Gwen prayed thru to the experience of being baptized with the Holy Ghost with the evidence of speaking in tongues. However, Gwen went further than that, cloven tongues of fire fell on her and she preached in tongues and then fell into a Pentecostal trance and her spirit left her body. Some people refer to this as being slain in the Spirit. She was visibly in a trance like state and no one could revive her. Everyone was concerned because she definitely was not faking it. She was as limp as a rag doll. Gwen was gone from her body and definitely not in the church where her body was.

There is a second Baptism that even the Holy Ghost filled people sometimes don't seek. That is the Baptism of Fire.

"I will baptize you with the Holy Ghost and Fire."

Gwen prayed and tarried till she was baptized with the Holy Ghost. Afterward she tarried and received the second promised Baptism of Fire. She left her body and looked down on the congregation and the Holy Ghost showed her visions just like John the revelator. After a series of visions, she returned to her body, spoke in tongues, and then opened her eyes. She arose from the altar a different woman and became a minister herself.

You never hear the Fire Baptism preached. However, it does exist and it is a stepping from your body experience and communing face to face with God and the Holy Ghost. John the revelator did it. Gwen is one of the few that I know of in the Pentecostal ranks that has experienced this. However, if we are true Pentecostals and have been baptized in the Holy Ghost with the evidence of speaking in tongues we should seek the Fire.

I have always heard the fire spoke of in terms of zeal to get out and preach the gospel or perform some sort of Christian duty. That is not the fire. That is zeal.

The fire of God is an experience, an out of body experience, of being able to be caught up to the throne just like John the revelator. It is a Baptism in the knowledge of Heaven. It is your soul being able to travel to the Father and speak with him and the Holy Ghost face to face. The Holy Ghost is a being.

I am a peeper. When my eyes should be closed, I can't help myself. I want to see the experiences others in the Pentecostal ranks are having. If I didn't peep, I would have nothing to write about. So, I guess you could say I am a Holy Ghost filled Peeping Tom.

I watched Gwen in her tarrying and then her receiving of the Holy Ghost. I also was there the night she left her body lying in a trance while she experienced the fire or being caught away to God. I was young and everything was exciting and of interest to me. While she was gone from her body I had the feeling that she had to be the most beautiful woman I had ever seen. There was something about her face that took on a look that was not of this world while she lay there in trance. I think now I was seeing a halo or God's aura around her. It could have been a sign of the Fire Baptism. her experience. Maybe a halo shining is a sign of the Fire Baptism just as speaking in tongues is the evidence of the Holy Ghost. I have over the years given the Fire Baptism much serious thought.

When service was over, and Sister Ette, the evangelist, dismissed the service; Gwen who was still red faced from her trance experience headed straight for me calling, "Wait!" I was headed out with my college aged friends, but I turned and waited.

With a serious look on her face like I have never seen on a Holy Ghost recipient she told me the following.

"I was out of my body. God and the Holy Ghost were showing me visions. One of them was about you."

"Really?" I asked in shock not really understanding why God would have any particular interest in me. I was just twenty two, a peeper, and young enjoying my friends.

"I saw Sister Ette preaching, but it was you in her shoes. She was not in her shoes. I saw you in front of the congregation instead of her."

"I was in shock and didn't know what to say. For one thing, I had felt no call to the ministry. I had tarried till I received the Holy Ghost but wasn't displaying any particular gift other than speaking in tongues.

Since then, I have come to realize that I do have a higher calling on my life and that is to write about and point people to the Baptism in Fire. Sister Ette pointed people to the infilling of the Holy Ghost. Standing in Sister Ette's shoes believing in the Holy Ghost I have taken one step further than her and what she preached. Back then the fire was never mentioned other than calling it zeal. I discovered thru Gwen's experience that the Baptism in Fire is a separate and second experience. I have walked in Sister Ette's shoes and now I walk beyond. The Bible promised Latter Rain is the second promised experience, the Baptism of Fire.

I am carrying the word that there is another Baptism and it is the Fire. I am standing like Sister Ette pointing the way. Thru my writing, I am probably able to reach as many, if not more people, than Sister Ette thru my writing. The Baptism in the Holy Ghost was the former rain. Now it is time for the Latter Rain, the Baptism of Fire, the catching away to God. Gwen was my forerunner, like John the Baptist, telling of my future coming. I come to you preaching with my pen telling you to seek the Fire, the catching away to God. The Fire Baptism is a step beyond Pentecostalism of the past and the infilling of the Holy Ghost.

Be caught up to God. Tarry till the Baptism in Fire and the Latter Rain falls on you. Tarry just like you did when you sought the infilling of the Holy Ghost.

I am a voice proclaiming that the Fire Baptism is a separate experience from the Holy Ghost and a higher experience intended for those of the End Time or end of the New Testament age. The Baptism of Fire and the Latter Rain is now. The catching away to God is now. Will you be left behind?

The End

Some of the experiences in this book are mine and others have been told to me by friends. I am a writer.

I am an old woman at the time of authoring this book. God breathed into me the breath of life in 1945. If you wish to share your stories and experiences concerning the Fire Baptism, please write. I am open to writing another book to point the way for those coming after me and you to a higher experience.

If you don't hear from me, just figure that I have left my human vessel and have put on new shoes to shout and dance all over God's Heaven!